CHECKMATE

CHECKMATE

NORAH LOFTS

ISIS
LARGE PRINT
Oxford

Copyright © Norah Lofts, 1975

First published in Great Britain 1975
by
Corgi

Published in Large Print 2010 by ISIS Publishing Ltd.,
7 Centremead, Osney Mead, Oxford OX2 0ES
by arrangement with
Author's Estate

The moral right of the author has been asserted

British Library Cataloguing in Publication Data
Lofts, Norah, 1904–1983.
  Checkmate.
  1. Victims of violent crimes - - Fiction.
  2. Parents with disabilities - - Fiction.
  3. Revenge - - Fiction
  4. Suspense fiction.
  5. Large type books.
  I. Title
  823.9'2–dc22

ISBN 978–0–7531–8564–3 (hb)
ISBN 978–0–7531–8565–0 (pb)

Printed and bound in Great Britain by
T. J. International Ltd., Padstow, Cornwall

Thursday January 18th

"*Blasted* evening classes!" Tom said. "Look at the time!"

Alice did not look up. She was knitting one of those huge, ridged sweaters for Jenny and the ridges took some making.

"Maybe the bus was late." Her voice was placid.

"I can check on that," he said, and with the dexterity of long practice, he swung his wheel-chair towards the table where the telephone stood. He dialled the number of the King's Head, in Overby. The bus from Chesford stopped and turned in the inn's forecourt.

His telephone manner was always brusque. It was one of the many things about him which misled people into thinking that he was a bad-tempered man — as who wouldn't be, afflicted as he was?

"Evening Mrs Beeson. Tom Penfold. Is the bus in? On time? Anybody there who was on it? Would you ask, then? Did anybody happen to notice my daughter?"

He waited, while above the murmurous noise, Mrs Beeson's useful voice bellowed the question.

"Thanks." He dropped the receiver and without turning said, "Three blind men and one who thought he saw her but couldn't be sure."

"Maybe she missed it."

"Then she'd be home by now. If she did what I told her and took a taxi. Alice, do you realise, she's twenty-two minutes late?" To comfort himself he added, "It's possible that Mrs Cooper asked her to bring something. She often does."

"But she's away," Alice said, placidly. The front door thudded, rather more softly than usual.

"There she is," Alice said and put down her knitting. She was first through the door into the hall.

Every door on the ground floor of this house had been designed for Tom's convenience; they opened this way, that way at a touch, and then closed of their own accord, rather slowly. Tonight, too slowly. Alice had time only to take one horrified glance, remember not to flap and to say in a fairly ordinary voice, "Hullo, dear," and then, there in the opening was Tom.

"My God! What happened to you?"

Jenny had wanted them not to know. She'd hoped to get up to the bathroom, see if her face looked as bad as it felt, see what an application of cold water would do before she faced them — her loving parents.

Reluctantly, she turned. Swollen mouth; swelling eye.

"I was mugged," she said and began to cry.

Alice ran up the five stairs Jenny had mounted and regardless of the mud on the blue anorak, on the long fair hair, put her arms around her daughter. "There, there," she said. "So long as you're not hurt. Never mind losing your bag. Come and tell us." She guided Jenny into the living-room.

Tom thought — That bloody lane! It was the idea of Jenny walking along it alone, after dark that had made

2

him so vehemently opposed to the evening classes. Always in the past and still on ordinary days, she walked to his office after school, had a cup of tea, did a bit of homework and then came home with him in the car; all safe and sound. But children grew up, became sixteen, had ideas and plans of their own; you couldn't protect them forever. And there was some truth in what Alice said — nowadays a country lane was safer than a busy city street.

Oh to be able to go out, chase the bastard, beat him up!

All that a man with useless legs could do was to splash a little brandy into a glass and say,

"Take a sip of that, honey. Don't cry, it's all over. He can't have got far. Did you see him?" He had given her a torch with a beam like a car's headlight; heavy, too; quite a weapon.

On a splutter and a sob, Jenny said, "It was an old tramp."

It was rather surprising that she even knew the name of this virtually extinct breed.

"All hairy, and raggy and smelly," Jenny said.

"Not . . . not Josh Salter?" Alice asked, naming their nearest neighbour, an old man with whom she had never felt really at ease though Tom seemed to like him and said he was simply eccentric.

"No. A tramp."

Tom was already at the telephone, dialling the big new Police Station in Chesford, being told to hold on, being told he would be put through and thinking nostalgically of the days of the old village bobby on a

3

bike, the man who would have known every barn, every stackyard, every empty house in which a vagrant was likely to hole up.

Holding the receiver, when at least he had made contact with somebody who sounded sensible, he said, "Honey, did you notice which way he went?"

"Down the lane," Jenny said. "Ramsfield way."

Tom relayed this information; pretty vital, for Ramsfield was only a hamlet; two farms, a few cottages and an old people's home. It was connected with the outer world by two lanes that made a kind of loop, diverging, and meeting again in Overby. Dove Lane, that was theirs, ran out from near the King's Head, and Shepherd's Lane led back to Overby church and green and village shop. A restricted area; one in which a hairy, dirty-smelling, ragged stranger would certainly be conspicuous.

Jenny's swollen lip was seeping blood; the bump below her left eye gave her face a lop-sided look. Still at the telephone table, Tom said, "I think old Shaw should take a look at you."

"Oh no! I'm not *hurt*, Dad. All I need is a bath."

"It's so late to call him out for something I can cope with," Alice said. After all, she had qualified as a nurse. "Come along, darling, I'll help you. Let's get that coat off." But Jenny clutched the anorak about her and said, "I can manage, Mum." She made quickly for the door. Alice was following her when she remembered that she also had a duty towards Tom. His face had the grey look which she associated with his bouts of pain. He'd had a shock.

Jenny had taken no more than two sips of the brandy, but her broken lip had smeared the edge of the glass. Use it for cooking, Alice thought, thriftily. She poured a rather larger quantity into a fresh glass and handed it to Tom, "Here, love, drink this and don't worry. She isn't hurt, that's the main thing." She was not dependent on alcohol herself, confining her drinking to a little sweet brown sherry on occasions, but there was no doubt about it, it helped Tom, and now that they knew that what he ate or drank could not affect his condition, why shouldn't he have what comfort he could find?

"One thing," he said, "that's the end of evening classes. Until she can drive."

Alice sensed rebuke, though none was intended. It was true that her failure to master a car added complications to their lives. And it was strange that she who never panicked in the ordinary way, once at the wheel of a car became nervous to the point of idiocy.

Upstairs Jenny was already in the bathroom, with the door locked.

Alice called. "What about supper? I've kept it hot."

"I don't want any."

"A hot drink then. Darling you must have something. Ovaltine or Horlick's."

"Oh, all right." She sounded impatient as well as ungrateful. "Ovaltine." The scent of rose geranium bath salts seeped on to the landing and followed Alice to the turn of the stairs.

Between the front door and the foot of the stairs was the hall window, and below it was a Victorian plant stand, kept for sentiment's sake and now again the latest fashion. It had belonged to Tom's mother, as had also the venerable aspidistra, another thing restored to favour. Alice had divided it many times, kept some of the young and given many away; but the mother-plant always had pride of place in the central, upmost level. Tonight it lay almost on its side; somebody must have pushed against it. Alice went to set it upright. And there, between the wall and the back of the stand was Jenny's bag.

It was blue, like most of Jenny's appendages; something started long ago by Tom "To go with your bonny blue eyes." It had been Tom's Christmas present, but naturally Alice had shopped for it, bearing in mind Jenny's warning. "Mum please, don't bring some home for him to choose from. His idea of a handbag is a miniature Gladstone with a snap. I want . . ." She knew exactly what she wanted and Alice had found it, not without difficulty, blue being an unfashionable colour this year.

Now she stood with it in her hands, incredulous, shocked for a moment into immobility. Then, with an anxious glance at the sitting-room door, she pushed it inside her cardigan and went back upstairs.

This time she did not call outside the closed door. She said, in a low but carrying voice, "Jenny, you must let me in. At once. I've found your bag!"

Jenny said bitterly, "You would!"

The door opened a little. Jenny stood there, huddled into a bath towel. Mingling with the scent of rose geranium was the scent of shampoo Jenny favoured. Clots of its froth rode on the surface of the bath water.

"All right," Jenny said, forestalling any question or reproach, "I told you a lie. Not to upset you. If you'd just given me a minute I could have said my torch failed and I'd run into a tree or something."

"What did happen, exactly? Jenny, you can tell *me*, surely."

"It wasn't a tramp. It was a terrible boy . . . a horrible, hateful . . ."

"Did he . . . assault you?"

Alice had spent the first ten years of her life in a Leicester slum, father a confirmed drunkard, mother an amateur prostitute, but not on the whole a bad parent. When she said, "Scram", Alice and the rest of them scrammed, knowing that presently reward would come, in the form of fish and chips.

Rape, prostitution — both kinds — and incest had been commonplace in her background until she was taken into care by the State and shown a new way of life. She had been smart enough to take advantage of it, and shrewd enough in later years, never to refer to her early youth; not even to Tom who knew only that she had been orphaned early and reared in a Children's Home.

Now those deliberately ignored, sordid years proved useful. Alice could not drive a car but she was equipped to deal with a situation which, pray God, Tom need never visualise. It was quite unnecessary for Jenny to say, "Dad mustn't know." Of course he mustn't know, he'd go mad!

"Trust me," Alice said, the humiliating business over. "I shan't say a word. It was awful for you, darling, but you're all right. And you must forget it."

"I never can."

"You can if you set your mind to it. These things happen — more often than we know; and people forget, I'll give you a couple of asplets and you'll sleep the clock round."

The doorbell — a set of musical chimes — sounded. The porch light had been left on for Jenny, and now shone upon a young, fresh-faced policeman. Tom welcomed him with the ease of one who has never been on the wrong side of the law. It was an attitude which Alice could never acquire. The police specialised in awkward questions. Her first thought was that Jenny and the policeman must not meet; Tom's was the reverse. By the time that Alice, moving rather slowly, joined them in the living-room, Tom was saying, "My daughter can give a pretty good description of the man, Sergeant." To Alice he said, "Call Jenny, my dear."

"I'm afraid I can't do that," Alice said, adopting her hospital manner. "She is, naturally, very shocked. She is under sedation." Then, answering the disappointment visible on both men's faces, she said quickly, "She gave me an exact description." She had enough presence of mind to be fair to Josh Salter. "He was short and thick-set, very dirty. Jenny said he stank. He had long hair and a beard and was wearing a ragged old army overcoat. Oh, and a broken bowler hat."

The police sergeant wrote diligently. Then he remarked, "She observed a good deal. In the time." Just the kind of thing a policeman would say, Alice thought.

"She carried a very good torch," Tom said. "As for time, she must have had quite a struggle. The bus was on time and she was a full twenty-five minutes late."

"Was she injured in the struggle?"

"He hit her on the mouth and on one eye," Tom said.

"And snatched her bag. Could you give me a description?"

Tom was capable of showing impatience, even with the police.

"Never mind that," he said, "get out, man, and find him."

Unruffled the sergeant said, "It could help to identify him, sir."

Tom described the bag, very accurately because he had looked at it critically, and disapproved though Alice had said it was the best she could find. It was not leather; plastic, and all over with brass studs, likely to tarnish in five minutes. A cheap affair, costing only £1.60. So he'd slipped in a five-pound note before presenting it. He remembered this now and mentioned it.

"Usually such people dispose of the bags as quickly as possible. But even today a vagrant changing a fiver might be noticed. It all helps." Pocketing his notebook, promising to let them know of any developments, Sergeant Bateson went away.

★ ★ ★

Knowing what she knew, and what Tom did not, made Alice feel uncomfortable with him.

"I've just remembered, I left Jenny's supper in the oven. I left the washing up, too, thinking I might as well do it altogether."

She went into the kitchen, but he followed, wiping dishes as she washed them, and talking and talking. Always, as was his way, comparing the present unfavourably with the past.

He wasn't all that old, only forty-six, but his affliction had aged him, so that he talked of the past as a very old man might do. Very old men harked back to the days they thought good because then they had been young and active. For the same reason Tom harked back to the time when he had been sound. Wiping a plate over and over, long after it was dry, he told Alice that civilisation was breaking down; it always began with the collapse of law and order. Twenty years ago, even ten, this kind of thing wouldn't have happened; Good God, he could remember when . . . And wasn't it a symptom of the times that the brute must be found with Jenny's bag on him? As though a description were not enough. "Scare her to death," he said vehemently, "smash her face, but unless he's got the bag, or the fiver, he'll be given the benefit of the doubt. And if they do arrest him, with the fiver on him, some old woman of a magistrate will say — Poor fellow, he was hungry. Give him a beefsteak."

She listened, concurred, the only thing to do when Tom was in this state, and was both relieved and agitated when the chimes rang again.

"I'll go," he said. The kitchen door sighed open. With incredible speed Tom shot his chair across the hall, managed the front door and had it open just before the kitchen door closed itself.

"Oh. Hullo, Salter. Come in . . ." Close as a shadow the lurcher bitch, Josh Salter's familiar, followed him in.

"I felt I oughta just ask if your girl was all right," Josh Salter said. "She got up and run, so I reckoned she wasn't hurt *much*. Then this silly old bitch went chasing off after the motor-bike. Clear into Overby. And I had had warning. So I chased after her. I mean, if I don't keep her under control, she's a goner, poor thing."

"You *saw* my daughter attacked?"

"No. What I seen was her getting up and running. So I reckoned she wasn't much hurt. And as I say, Gyp here went off after the bike. *And*, she nailed him. No denying that. There's blood on her muzzle. See for yourself." Tom looked. The lurcher was a darkish brindle, going white around eyes and muzzle; there were some darkening streaks.

"Gyp bit the tramp?" My God, I hope badly. I hope to the bone.

"What tramp, Mr Penfold? Are we talking about the same thing?"

"I'm talking about the tramp who attacked my daughter. This evening in the lane. He hit her, knocked her down, took her bag."

11

"But why? He's all right for money. His silly old Moo of a mother sees he's all right."

"Who?"

"That young villain on the bike. Upworth. The funny thing is, she took against him from the start. I reckon he must've kicked her. And talk about elephants . . ."

Elliptical, evasive, maddening! He lived alone, probably talked to himself, or to the dog and didn't bother to be coherent.

"Have a drink?" Tom asked.

"Very welcome, Mr Penfold. Very welcome. I had to run pretty hard and I ain't as spry as I once was."

Whisky! A bonus, except at Christmas. The old man helped occasionally in the garden and was paid, but also rewarded with beer, a bit of chat and what he liked to think of as friendship from Tom if not from his missus who always seemed a bit wary of Josh and a bit scared of Gyp.

"Now," Tom said. "Tell me what you saw and what you heard. Begin at the beginning."

"Well, it was last summer," the infuriating old man began. "Mrs Cooper had that do in her garden and some bad types turned up. On motor-bikes. Gyp didn't like them — she never did — so she give chase, and as I say, I reckon young Upworth kicked her. And she never forgot. He've been down the lane two-three times since and she always knew and raised Cain. So tonight he went by, and she raised Cain, wouldn't even eat her supper. Nice bit of rabbit it was, too. But she quieted and afterwards, a good bit afterwards, she asked to go out. Very clean she is."

The lurcher knew that she was being talked about; her ears twitched, she kept her lucent, amber gaze fixed on her master. Tom set his teeth, clenched his hands and sweated with impatience.

"So I let her out, see, and off she went like a shot; *down* the lane. This way. I called to her. Then I saw something going on. And as I say, I seen your girl get up and start to run. But young Upworth, he jump on his bike and tear off towards Overby, Gyp after him, and me after her."

"You didn't see a tramp?"

"There weren't nobody in the lane except your girl, young Upworth, me. And Gyp, here."

"Was it light enough to see?"

"Yes, the moon was up. Added to which, if it'd been a black as Newgate's knocker, I'd have known by the way she carried on."

"Well," Tom said, "that casts new light ... And whether he robbed Jenny or not, he assaulted her; her face is badly bruised. And you are a witness."

Suddenly Josh Salter looked profoundly uneasy. He took a big, unappreciative swig at his whisky and said,

"I never seen what he did, Mr Penfold. And if you're thinking of making a case ... It wouldn't stick. Rate he was going he'd be in Stan's Caff in under the quarter hour, with a lot of his pals as'd swear he'd been there since six. See? Who'd take my word?"

"You said Gyp bit him."

"Kerist! So I did!" What showed of the old man's face, between beard, whiskers and shaggy eyebrows

13

took on the colour of sea-sickness. But he was a hardy old man and his voice and manner were under control.

"Well, we must be off. I reckoned I just oughta ask."

There was no need for him to call Gyp; as he stood up, she rose and took her place by his side.

Tom was controlled too; he managed to say,

"I'm infinitely obliged to you, Salter. And to Gyp. But for you something worse might have happened."

Had it happened?

Why else should Jenny concoct such a story?

"All in a day's work," Josh Salter said. "Don't bother yourself, Mr Penfold. I can let myself out. Goodnight."

He let himself out with the maximum speed, and once outside broke into a shambling trot and did not pause until he reached his near-derelict cottage. There he collected his Post Office Savings Book and Gyp's licence and raked out what remained of his fire. Fastening on the dogs collar and lead, he said, "Time to make ourselves scarce for a bit, old dear." Mentioning Terror Upworth's ability to manufacture an alibi had reminded him that he had contacts in Leicester where poached game had a ready market. There were people there who would gladly swear that he and Gyp had been in their company on Thursday, the 18th of January or any other date he cared to name. Respectable fellows too. Cut through the woods, thus avoiding Overby; hop a lorry on the main road, and Bob's your uncle.

★ ★ ★

Alice — and her state of mind could have been judged by any really impartial observer, by the fact that she had not removed her apron — came in just as Tom was being told once more to hold on, and that he would be put through. Waiting, holding the receiver, he said, "My dear, Salter has just told me something that does not agree with Jenny's account. It wasn't a tramp . . . Hullo there! Yes, I *am* holding on . . . Alice it was a boy. Salter recognised him."

Alice looked sea-sick, but she also showed self-control, though what she did was extraordinary. She took the receiver from Tom's hand and dropped it into its cradle. "Tom, don't be hasty. Just listen to me, *please*. Let's not have the police in on this. For Jenny's sake . . ."

"But I know the lout's name. I know where he is at this minute. And he's marked. Salter's dog bit him."

"It'd mean hundreds of questions. And she'd have to identify him. Think how she'd feel. And nothing would happen to him. They'd simply blame her."

"For being *attacked*?"

"They always blame the girl, Tom. And though they don't print names in the paper, it always gets out somehow. People'd know and say it was her fault for associating with people like . . ." Just too late she saw where earnestness had led her.

"Like who, Alice?"

She faltered. "You said a boy, Tom. A lout . . ."

"Another second and you'd have named him, wouldn't you? What has she told you? And why did she tell us that pack of lies?"

"She . . . she didn't want to upset you."

"Fetch her down."

"I can't. She's asleep, or at least in no state . . . Dad, please, leave it alone. Let her get over it in her own way. What she said was for your sake. Let her think . . . Tom, you know I never argue with you, or ask for anything much, now I do beg you, I beg you, leave it alone . . ."

With every word she spoke his suspicion darkened. He remembered Alice's slippery streak. Nothing much, just, in the early days of their marriage, little evasions, all intended to shift blame; and natural enough, he had thought — being in love with her — in a girl who had passed from the discipline of the Children's Home to that of the Hospital; a girl who had an inbuilt desire to please. He'd always been very gentle with her, and he was gentle now.

"Alice, you must see that I have to know the truth. Fetch her down."

"Tom, I can't. At least leave it till tomorrow."

He gave his chair a thrust that carried it through the door, into the hall and across to the foot of the stairs. There he shouted,

"Jenny! Jenny! Come down here. I want a word with you."

Jenny came.

He had always adored her and it would have been only a slight exaggeration to say that she had shaped his life. When this mysterious thing happened to him, some obscure form of paralysis, something nobody understood, or could arrest, he could have given way, become one of the helpless, to whom the State was very kind. He'd had a little money — the vast firm which had employed him was prepared to give him a pension; Alice could make pin-money doing a few hours casual work in the nearest hospital. And he would have rotted. But for Jenny. It was for her sake — drowning men clutch at any straw — that he had heaved himself up, overcome so far as possible, his disability, gambled his all in setting up in business for himself, become not a poor old father to be pitied, but one whom any rational girl could respect as well as love.

He considered her beautiful, which she was not; the bonny blue eyes which he joked about were too pale, so was her skin; only her hair saved her from being rather colourless. It would darken or dim with time, but now it was truly the colour of fresh-run honey. She had also a certain languishing grace, a delicate, rather precious air which could be appealing or infuriating according to the feeling of the beholder — it infuriated gym mistresses and others of the brisker type.

Even now, about to hold the necessary inquisition, Tom thought that she looked like a lily, too roughly handled.

"Honey," he said, "I'm sorry to bring you down. But there's something I must know."

Mum, of course! Witless, guileless woman. And false! Swearing not to tell and then coming straight down and blurting everything out.

Alice had in fact caught her daugher's eye and made a grimace that might have conveyed anything; warning, despair, resignation. And now, anxious to exonerate herself — and to show Jenny how the land lay, she said quickly,

"Darling, Josh Salter has been in. His story didn't quite agree . . ."

"I see."

Perhaps it was the swollen lip, but her voice seemed to have changed.

"Honey, why did you make up that tale?"

"To spare you. I didn't want you upset."

There was nothing more calculated to rouse Tom's ire than any hint, any implication that he needed protection or consideration, simply because his legs were useless.

"I *am* upset. Anybody would be. Your story upset me. Salter's upset me even more. What I want to know is why *you* told a lie to protect a young savage."

"I knew you'd make a fuss. It wouldn't have done me any good. And you a lot of harm."

"How? Where's the difference between your being set upon by a tramp, or by a lout?"

"There is a difference," Jenny said.

Within her reach there was a long, low table bearing the big silver cigarette box presented to Tom by his colleagues upon his "retirement", premature and enforced, but ritually marked. From it Jenny took a cigarette.

Alice didn't really approve of smoking. Tom was an addict; he'd smoke anything, a cigarette, a pipe, a cigar. His habits were fixed long before he'd married her; she had however registered a mild protest when, about a year ago, she'd found Tom not encouraging exactly, but not forbidding Jenny the occasional cigarette. She had spoken about lung cancer and Tom had made one of the remarks that she thought flippant. "Poor old brother Nicotine! Now being blamed for the decline in tuberculosis!" She'd asked, "How do you make that out?" And Tom had explained. Everybody ever born had to die of something, some failure of physical structure or function. The clever ones had practically eliminated tuberculosis and substituted lung cancer as the bogey.

So now Jenny took a cigarette, worked the lighter with unsteady fingers, inhaled, exhaled and explained, in a cold, distant way.

"If I could just have got upstairs . . . Nobody need have known. I was caught, and I lied. I knew that if you knew you'd make a fuss. And then the gang would move in. Wreck your car. Set fire to the Works. You have no idea . . . He's very bad, and very powerful."

"A boy named Upworth?"

"Yes. Terry; known as the Terror."

"Do you know him, Jenny?"

"In a way."

"What does that mean?"

"Mrs Cooper's thing in aid of Oxfam ended with a dance. He and some of the gang turned up. He wanted to bring me home on the back of his bike. I lied to him, too. I said I was at home and walked into the house. Then one day he was waiting outside the school, offering me a lift. I was with Kate and I said I was going to tea with her. He's waited since then, too, dogging

19

me. Mostly, nowadays I leave by the side gate, into the Park. That's all."

She disgorged this information unwillingly and with distaste.

Alice interposed swiftly, "Really, Dad, I think she's had enough for one day. *And* two asplets."

"And tonight, Honey?"

"Waiting in the lane. This," she pointed to her lip and sneered, "is a kiss from Terry Upworth! And this is what you get for resisting. He's dangerous. And if you go making a fuss, he'll hurt you too. Ask Dr Anders if you don't believe me."

"How does Anders come into this?"

Jenny stubbed out her cigarette — rather too carefully before she answered.

"I don't quite know. It was something . . . something between Terry and Colin Anders, and Dr Anders was all for taking action. But the gang either did something, or threatened something that made him think again. Anyway, nothing happened. I know through Kate."

To Tom, who had not moved with the times, it seemed strange that the son of Chesford's highly respectable doctor and the daughter of the town's highly respected solicitor should be mentioned, almost in the same breath as a youth whom even that old reprobate, Josh Salter, described as a villain. Kate Dawson was Jenny's best friend, and often with her and her family Jenny had enjoyed trips and holidays which a chairbound man could not share.

"How does Kate come into this?"

20

"She and Colin are very friendly — at least, they were. But it is true. Terry's dangerous."

"And will continue to be if people are too scared . . . Look here, Jenny, *we're* not scared, are we? You're a sensible girl; you can take a wider view. If he isn't checked, what happened to you will happen to other girls. You wouldn't mind telling the police what happened, and identifying him if necessary. Would you, Honey?" His voice was almost coaxing.

"Yes, I would," Jenny said violently. "Because I know just what would happen. He'd produce some girls who'd swear that I'd been running round with him for ages, that I had a date with him in the lane. Everybody'd say I got no more than I asked for. He'd blacken my name and then move in on you. Start a strike or something."

"Honey you over-estimate him. There isn't a better, more loyal, happier work force in England."

He had reason to believe that. He had fanatical views about the relationship between management and staff. Properly handled, there was no workman like the British workman. When he said that he knew what he was talking about, in his good days he'd worked in Iran, Kenya, Brazil; always on vast projects. A man in a wheel-chair must cut his coat according to his cloth, and Penfold's at Chesford manufactured what were loosely called Component Parts. Tom knew every man he employed by name, by family history. He knew every job quite as well as, sometimes better than, the fellow who was doing it. Every day he ate his midday meal in the canteen — never at a separate table so that food of

21

differing quality could be served — he knew all the tricks and was the first to complain. He was not paternalistic; he never kidded himself that his men were personally devoted to him — though there was a tendency to give boy babies the name of Thomas. What he had made, from small beginnings, was a workable machine; just as he had made a workable way of life for himself; in this house.

"This and this," Jenny said, again touching her lip, her eye, "will be better tomorrow. Please, Dad, forget it. I don't want to be asked a lot of questions, and have lies told about me. All to no purpose."

She was being logical — as he had, bit by bit, taught her to be. She wasn't pleading, as Alice had done, saying, "I beg you". She was his daughter. He thought that she could stand another question, very personal, very piercing. How to put it?

He said, "Before I make a decision, Jenny, tell me this. Would there be any truth in what he would say in his defence — that you had dallied, flirted with him. Don't be afraid to say so. I know that rogues often do have a peculiar attraction . . ."

"I hated him, from the first moment. And I was scared of him, too. And if you won't listen or understand . . . If you must go ahead and make a fuss, I shall kill myself. I'd rather be dead than dragged through the mud and labelled as one of his sluts!"

Her voice was suddenly shrill and her eyes wild.

"Dear," Alice said, "you mustn't talk like that. Tom, I told you she was in no fit state . . ." She rose and stood in front of Jenny. "Come along now, into bed with you."

22

When Alice returned to the living-room, Tom was sitting where she had left him, a brooding, heavy look on his face. She made her little preparations for bed; placed the guard in front of the fire, emptied ashtrays, put her knitting in its bag, collected and folded the newspapers and all the time waiting for Tom to speak, so that she might assess and comply with his mood. She was grateful that the questioning had stopped where it did, grateful that Jenny's wild statement had given her obvious cause to intervene; grateful, too, that the wild statement so fully backed up her own argument.

"There's a lot in this I don't like, Alice," he said abruptly.

"We none of us like it. It's a horrid thing to have happened. The less made of it, the better."

"I wish I could be sure of that . . . Did you notice how . . . how *slippery* she was as soon as Kate Dawson was mentioned? I did. And all that rubbish about a strike at the Works. There's a smack of something . . . You heard her say that if she could have got upstairs nobody'd have known anything. Alice, is that the normal behaviour of a girl who'd just been attacked? She didn't get upstairs, so she made up the tramp story. That fell down. And by that time she'd got another story. But the aim of both was the same — protection of Terry Upworth. Why, Alice, why?"

"Well, she did explain that. She was concerned for you."

"A load of old rubbish! That wasn't our Jenny. She didn't even sound like herself. I don't mean just at the end when she said she'd . . . I mean all along. Cagey. Keeping something back."

"She'd had a shock, Tom. And she was half-doped." Alice was anxious to get away, go to bed, take a couple of asplets herself and put a night's sleep between herself and this shocking evening. She had suffered the additional strain of preserving an outward show of imperturbability. But dutiful still she said, "Would you like me to help you tonight, darling?"

Startled, Tom said, "No thank you. I can still get myself to bed, thank God." He looked at the telephone. "I'm not sure, Alice. I still think this should be reported. I can't stomach the idea of that young thug getting off scot-free."

"You heard what Jenny said."

"She didn't mean it."

"I wouldn't be too sure. Sixteen is a tricky age. Don't forget Julia Walpole."

"Neurotic as hell. Jenny isn't like that."

A thought stabbed. An hour ago he would have said that Jenny was incapable of lying. He'd always been insistent upon the truth, explaining that whatever it was, whatever had happened, honesty would make up for, while deceit would compound the fault. As a result, with nothing to fear, she had grown up to be very honest. Besides, she trusted him; they had enjoyed a singularly good relationship — until tonight.

Another, even sharper stab!

He said, "Alice! Do you think it possible that he *raped* her?"

Too quickly Alice said, "Oh, no, Tom. No!"

But if he didn't know Jenny, he knew Alice. That scarlet blush, that inability to meet his eye — signs of something he'd thought over and done with.

"How can you be so sure?"

The too ready answer. "She would have told me, wouldn't she? Her own mother!"

Something seemed to click inside his head; he felt, of a sudden, very ill.

Somewhere along the long line of specialists in this and that there'd been a man whom Tom had deliberately tried *not* to remember. He was the one who had used the words, "possibly progressive". He had also warned against over-exertion, physical or mental, and above all against any kind of emotional excitement. He was the one who would have condemned Tom Penfold to the life of a slowly-rotting cabbage, tenderly cared for by gardeners intent only on the problem of keeping a carcass alive. Tom had defied him, proved him wrong, year after year; tremendous mental and physical efforts; plenty of emotional excitement — if that meant anger when things went wrong, or joy over a contract that meant work for a hundred men for the next three years. Now, with disconcerting abruptness, Tom realised what the man had meant. Emotional!

Alice thought — Poor Tom! Just to ask that question wrenched him; but I gave the right answer, didn't I? And it had worked.

Tom said, "Well, we'd better get to bed."

"And you'll take a pill — not lie awake, fretting." She owed him that much consideration because he had accepted her lie. As though in reward to her something flashed in his face, something that had been missing for years; bright, confident, young. It was only a flash and she had hardly time to think that it was incongruous on a middle-aged face, scored with lines of pain, of endurance, concentration.

"I shan't fret, Alice."

As was customary they parted at the foot of the stairs, with a chaste, but fond kiss. Their sex life — good while it lasted — had ended with Tom's disability. Alice had not felt much deprivation. Different as it was, as Tom was, as she was, the act itself had always been for her associated with old days, with a background where a virgin meant a girl over six years old who could run faster than her uncle, father, brother — not to mention boys on the street; or where complaisance was sometimes advisable; sixpence; a bar of chocolate; an orange. With Tom, of course, different, because she had loved him, been terribly, terribly grateful to him for all he had given her, the wedding ring, the jump in status, the courtesy, the love. But she had, for the last ten or more years, been happily content to sleep by herself, in a wide bed, cool in summer, warm in winter; with a lamp conveniently placed so that she could read, if she wished to, one of the magazines she favoured, or listen to her radio. Quite often she fell asleep to the sound of music and woke to a voice forecasting the day's weather or reporting the price of cabbages at Covent Garden.

On her way to her rest at the end of this horrid but — on the whole — rather well-managed evening, Alice looked in upon Jenny. There was enough light from the landing to show her the girl asleep.

Tom wheeled himself to his own part of the house; a sizeable room with an adjoining bathroom. The room contained, besides the bed, a small workbench, a desk, a bookcase, a chest-of-drawers and a cupboard fitted as a wardrobe, all set at a level within reach of a man in a wheel-chair. The bed was flanked by a sturdy steel bar by means of which he could heave himself in and out. Similar ones in the bathroom enabled him to take a brief shower, to use the lavatory. A man's legs might fail him, but while he had the use of his arms, and his head he could still be independant.

Every move was, of necessity, planned to be economical of effort. A kind of time-and-motion study in miniscule. With concentration he looked to put himself to bed, neatly and efficiently, within fifteen minutes. Tonight it took longer because . . . Because his concentration failed. It was because he was not thinking that his toothbrush fell from his hand and the coat hanger holding his jacket and waistcoat tilted, letting the garments slide to the bottom of the cupboard. He admitted that his hands were not as steady or sure as usual — but what man's would be, after such an experience? He would have repudiated, with the utmost vehemence, with oaths, that he was no longer quite the man he had been at twenty-five minutes past nine that evening.

Friday, January 19th

"Miss Jenny not coming?" Jack Rogers asked.

"No. She's got a bit of a cold."

"All mine are down with it." The blanket term was proof of the man's sterling good nature; he'd married a woman with two children, begotten two of his own, and then taken in two of his wife's sister's when they were deserted. He made absolutely no distinction between them.

Apart from Jenny's absence all was as usual. Jack came down the lane on his ramshackle bicycle, opened the garage and edged the car alongside the little glass-roofed shelter outside the kitchen door. The car was fitted with one of the steel hand-holds that were so important in the life of a handicapped man. By it Tom heaved himself in, and before slamming the door, lifted in his brief-case.

Breakfast had not been as usual. Alice had said, "She's still asleep. The best thing. Anyhow she couldn't possibly go . . ."

"Of course not." No further reference to Jenny, or to the events of the previous evening had been made.

Now Tom said, "Pull in at Salter's, will you Jack? I want a word with him."

When the first fairly rousing knock elicited no response, Tom said, "Knock harder."

"Bring the place down," Jack said with a grin; but he knocked louder and waited. "Must be away. Even if he was sleeping it off his old dog would have created."

"No matter," Tom said. But it did, because Tom had been counting upon the old man to give him a lead.

Try another way.

Where the lane debouched into the main road they had to wait while six enormous vehicles thundered past.

"Ought to be on the railways," Jack said. And that was routine too; he said it almost every morning.

Once they were edged into the traffic's flow, Tom said,

"Jack, does the name Upworth mean anything to you?"

"Builder, you mean? Yep. Sure. 'S'matter of fact, he's a sort of second cousin to Evie's first. Did very well for hisself, started out with one ladder and a paint brush, you might say, and ended up at Stapleford Hall. All done honestly, too, which is more than you can say for some."

"He has a son, I believe."

"'S'right. Pity about him."

"In what way?"

"Didn't settle to the business. Spoilt rotten, of course. Then there was some sort of rumpus and Terry got the boot. Set hisself up in a garridge, if you can call it that. Bad position, in Summerfield Road."

Summerfield Road was the one by which Tom had entered and left Chesford for ten years. Despite its pleasant name it was a stretch of squalid, urban sprawl. Cheap cafés, unprosperous-looking shops, a hideous junk yard full of disintegrating cars, all dominated by a Greyhound Stadium whose paint, once bright purple, was peeling and leprous. A few surviving trees stood knee deep in litter. It was a stretch of the journey from which Tom habitually averted his eyes.

"There you are," Jack said, slowing down slightly. "See what I mean. Wrong side of the road. People coming out of town have filled up at Thompson's or Blake's; people coming in don't want to cut across the traffic. Poor old Corder did his best but it beat him in the end."

Tom's eye took a photographic flash. Behind the forecourt was a small, pebble-dashed house, once white, now darkened and stained. It had an extension, mainly of glass before its front door; some panes were broken; behind others hung cards advertising SNACKS and various soft drinks. There was a workshop to one side, its wide doors closed. That somebody had at some time past done his best to make the place attractive was evidenced by the concrete troughs which separated the forecourt from the street, and wide, shallow bowls on either side of the door. Nobody expected floral displays in January, but there was a desolate look about the clotted weeds. There were two petrol pumps, one offering the brand Tom favoured, the other intended for lorries. Excrescences in the asphalt of the forecourt, rather like close-cut tree stumps, showed where others had been.

"Yes," Tom said. "I see what you mean. Run down."

Jack accelerated gently. He was a splendid driver. Once it had amazed Tom that anyone could drive so well without having the slightest idea about the mechanical processes which went on inside; but he was used to it now.

"Evie's got an idea that Daphne — that's his mum — sneaks him a bit on the sly. Any mother would, I s'pose."

A possible mine of information seemed to offer itself but Tom refrained from exploring it. Better not show too much interest.

It was a day much like any other, except that he found it difficult to keep his mind on the business. That was unusual; work had been his life-buoy, through pain, through anxious times. Today it failed him, his mind kept slipping back to the events of the previous evening, to his night thoughts and the decision he had almost taken. Almost! Once or twice he eyed the telephone broodingly, but the very viciousness of the charge he must bring deterred him. Alice had said "No" to the word rape, but Alice was not to be trusted; and if a prosecution concerning assault would embarrass the victim, how much worse would be the investigation of a more serious offence?

At the Works he used an electrically propelled chair in which he was fully mobile. Trying to escape his thoughts he whizzed about even more briskly than usual; and was careless once. The man operating the machine cried, "Be careful!" Tom snarled, "I was being careful, Stokes, when you were sucking titty." It was unlike the boss to be careless, and he didn't often snarl. Poor bastard didn't look very well; probably had a bad night. Stokes had the apt, ready answer. "I was bottle-reared, sir." Tom rewarded him with a grin. "And you're a good advertisement for it."

He'd made some show of eating his breakfast to please Alice whose impenetrable placidity had resumed control. Jenny had been mentioned only once. But the vacant place at table ached and the thing they did not talk about pervaded the atmosphere, like the stench of a blocked drain. It tainted the food.

He made some show of eating his lunch; the canteen cook, a miracle-worker who cooked for a hundred as well — and apparently as easily — as she would have cooked for four, had a sharp eye and had he not cleared up his salt beef and dumplings would have asked was anything wrong? The taint wasn't actually *here*, but the good food was tasteless; he had to choke it down.

By afternoon one problem was at least partially settled. Too late now to take the ordinary, good citizen's course. A man whose daughter had been raped wouldn't wait until afternoon of the next day. And why did you delay, Mr Penfold? Because my wife and my daughter told lies. No! My way is best.

He had a splendid secretary, Doris. Despite her appearance, she was lean and saturnine, she had a motherly nature. She would have mothered him, had she been allowed.

As usual, at a quarter past four she produced a tea-tray, daintily set, with the buttered buns which — so long ago as to seem prehistoric, Jenny had eagerly snatched at, eagerly devoured.

"Jenny won't be coming," he was obliged to say. "She's having a day off; a bit of a cold."

"Oh dear, I *am* sorry. I hope it isn't 'flu. There is a lot of it about. And if you don't mind my saying so, Mr Penfold, I think you look a bit under the weather." That was bold of Doris. Tom's well-being, or lack of it was a forbidden subject. Lots of men liked to be fussed over. The top drawer of Doris's typing table was almost a First Aid box, aspirin, Bandaid plasters, lozenges for sore throats, for coughs, antiseptic ointments.

"I'm all right," Tom said. He lifted the teapot. Heavier than usual, or his hand a little less sure. Fortunately Doris did not notice. She said, "I'll just pop out, if I may. Shan't be a minute."

When she came back she carried a white paper cone; nesting inside it a bunch of those frail, pale, sickly scented jonquils, over-forced for market in winter.

"Please give her these, Mr Penfold, and tell her I hope she'll soon be better."

"Really, Doris, you shouldn't . . ." He smiled, he tried to look pleased; but there was something about the pallid, wilting flowers . . . "Thanks a lot. Get hold of Jack for me, will you? I think I'll call it a day."

"Very wise," Doris said. "You go to bed, Mr Penfold, with a hot drink and a hot bottle and a couple of aspirin. And if you don't feel better in the morning . . .

There's nothing much pending. Just Mr Parker, from IMC. Higgins can deal with him."

My dear girl, Tom thought, how little you know! I am about to take the first hurdle. In a very peculiar obstacle race.

"She needs a fill-up," Jack said, veering towards Blake's. "I should've brought her round before, but there wasn't time. We're a mite early."

"How about trying that place — Corder's was it? — that you pointed out to me this morning." He hoped he sounded casual enough.

"Young Upworth's?" Dismay and disapproval rang in Jack's voice. "I hope you didn't pay no heed to what I said about him being a kind of connection of Evie's first. They ain't even friendly. Never was."

"The thought never occurred to me. I noticed the KL pump. And the place looked as though it could use a bit of custom."

And that, Jack thought, was the boss all over; making out to be a man of iron, and soft as putty really.

"We might save time too."

It was true that cars were lining up at Blake's. It was also true that the place was offering treble Yellow Stamps this week. Blazing hell!

Jack hoped that the "Closed" sign would be out at Corder's. It often was, even in business hours. He hoped there'd be a thundering great lorry filling up: lorries didn't mind cutting across traffic — nobody argued with a six-wheeler. In either event he could drive on to the roundabout, turn and go back to Blake's and take advantage of the Yellow Stamp offer.

Corder's was open, its forecourt empty; and service was brisk. The Yeoman was hardly in position before the door of the kiosk opened and the boy came out. He was smoking, but he dropped the cigarette and ground it underfoot.

Triggered by loathing, Tom's eye took a photographic flash. Upworth did not look like a thug. In fact he was good-looking and well-dressed. He was fairly tall, very well built and he moved gracefully. His hair was reddish-brown, properly cut and groomed; his face was clean shaven. He wore chestnut coloured corduroy slacks, a tawny polo-neck sweater, a brown sheepskin jacket, brown brogue shoes. His right hand was liberally criss-crossed with adhesive plaster. Gyp had nailed him all right.

Not in the least what Tom had expected; not — anyway at first glance — a young man to rouse instant distaste and fear in any girl; quite the contrary in fact.

He went to the driver's side of the car and Jack indicated by a jerk of his thumb that here the passenger did the ordering. Terry noticed the steel bar. A friend of his had once worked at Blake's and had mentioned the contraption. He was therefore able to say, "Good afternoon, Mr Penfold. How many, sir?" Not a bad voice, either; the accent local, but educated local. Product of Broadfield, Tom surmised, thinking of the nearby school, held to be almost as expensive as Eton.

"Eight." He wondered that he could speak at all, such conflicting thoughts assailed him. Renewed suspicion of Jenny's story; surprise; sheer curiosity; a wish to do violence; an awareness of the need for caution. Above and beyond all the thought that this young male body had, however briefly, possessed Jenny's, last night, in the mud. Even if she had flirted a bit — Tom tended to think in old-fashioned terms — that should not have happened. The wish to do violence took charge. *If only I could, for five minutes, be given back the use of my legs, I'd smash you to pulp.*

He held out a five-pound note with a hand that trembled. *Guard against emotional stress.* But who could? Could even that dismal, dessicated little man, if he had a daughter and she'd been . . .

Upworth produced change. Also a wet sponge with which he wiped the windscreen. *Service with a smile.* Seen at close quarters he was not quite so good-looking; something ferretty about the face, the forehead too narrow, steep, slightly receding, the mouth too thin-lipped. His eyes were light hazel, a pleasant colour in itself, just right with that hair, with those clothes, but rather protuberant; too much white showing.

"Had an accident?" Tom asked.

"Nothing much. Jacking up an old car, rotten with rust. Just a scrape." *Just a lie!*

"You do repairs?"

"I do. Or I should say, 'we'. I'm pretty handy, though I never trained. I have a man who is fully qualified."

Past the roundabout, out on to the road to Overby, they drove in silence. Jack broke it.

"This mean you're ditching Blake's?" He grieved over the loss of the Yellow Stamps, and he had been affronted by the windscreen wiping. He was no mechanic, but he did pride himself that the Yeoman was well kept outwardly as any car in the district.

Tom emerged from the tangled skein of thought.

"Not necessarily. I thought we might give this other place a try. Blake's is always busy."

"Busy or not, they never let you down yet, Mr Penfold. In fact they allust gave you priority, knowing what your car meant to you."

Ordinarily the remark, perfectly justified, holding in its heart the acknowledgement of his inability to use any other car, to take a taxi, clamber on to a bus, would have infuriated him. This afternoon he had more to think of.

"Jack, you sound disgruntled. Have you anything against young Upworth?"

"Evie don't like gossip. Like I said, the families ain't even friendly. But Evie's first's mother was born Upworth. Women are a bit sentimental . . . But his Mum knew, nylon stocking or no nylon stocking. And so did his Dad. The last straw as they say — and all hushed up as it was, young Terry got the order of the boot. With Upworth and Son on every lorry, every ladder. I ain't concerned, Mr Penfold, with what he did or didn't do. Let 'em chew their own bacon. What mattered to me was the Yellow Stamps."

"Yellow Stamps?"

"Blake's give 'em; we collect 'em. Evie's got her eye on a Kitchen Boy — dishwashing machine. Eight is a lot to wash up for, day in day out."

Concentrate on this for a moment; give your mind a respite.

"How many do you need?"

"I dunno. Evie keeps count. Thousands and thousands. Stampwise it's the most expensive thing in the catalogue. She reckoned that with a mite of luck she might get it by Christmas."

"And Christmas is a long way away."

"It is that. But I did notice this afternoon, just a bit lighter. We're heading in the right direction." His undefeatable cheerfulness was breaking through; he could never cherish a grudge or a grievance for long.

They turned into the lane. Mrs Cooper's imposing gateway with its two little lodges, almost opposite Josh Salter's hovel.

Somewhere about here! Last night. The mental vision had more clarity now that he'd seen the young brute.

"Jack, I've been thinking . . . You've been with me ten years."

"Goddlemighty. As long as that? Gone like a flash."

"I had been wondering what to give you to mark the occasion. Would you like a what was it? Kitchen Boy?"

"Mr Penfold, there's no call. Just because I chewed the rag a bit. Set you back between eighty and ninety pounds."

"I could get it cost price. Installed free. And Evie could have it tomorrow."

"I can just see her face!" He could also see the variety of things which the stamps already hoarded could obtain for the kids. The only drawback to a family like this was that there were always two, sometimes three, wanting the same thing at the same time. Then a thought struck him.

"What about the others?"

"What others?"

"I ain't the only one been with you ten years."

"True enough, and I can't give Kitchen Boys to them all. I tell you what, though, nose about a bit and try to find out something they hanker for. Up to ten pounds a head, say."

"No need to ask," Jack said promptly. "They'd like the lolly."

"They shall have it. Don't you go saying anything about the Kitchen Boy. After all nobody else is as important to me as you are."

"Anything I do for you, Mr Penfold is a pleasure. And thanks very much."

This should have been a happy little interlude. In addition to being naturally generous, Tom enjoyed being successful. Component Parts had got off to a wobbly start; converting the house to meet his needs had been an expensive business. Three of those ten years now to be celebrated had been haunted by bills and overdrafts. But he'd weathered through and could afford to give this decent fellow a Kitchen Boy.

"Jenny not down?"

Better not make too much of it, Alice thought.

"She did come down around lunch-time. But she seemed a bit limp and looked a bit pale, so I sent her back to bed."

Anxiety came uppermost. "I still think we should have the doctor."

"That'd be making too much of it. He'd ask questions and bring it all back. What she needs is rest and quiet and a chance to forget."

Alice also had had an unhappy day. Tom had asked that penetrating question and she had told him a thumping lie, which he had seemed to accept. But with Tom you never knew. He was, in his own way, a very secretive man. Not a liar, she could not remember a single occasion on which he had ever told her even a half-lie; but he did none the less, work in the dark, like a mole. And he chose his time. For instance he had everything planned, for the house in which they lived, the Works which was their sustenance, before he told her the final verdict — that he would never walk again. A man who could keep such a thing to himself, for weeks and weeks . . .

Breakfast had been a bit of an ordeal, and she had dreaded his homecoming. Now here he was, and early. She put out a smokescreen of activity. "Darling, you're early. I haven't even started the potatoes. But the fire's going . . . Oh how sweet, I must put them into water at once." She opened the paper cone. The slightly sickly sweet scent streamed out and Tom realised that it had been present as he took stock of his enemy, and during his chat with Jack — which should have been so pleasant and was not.

40

"Doris sent them."

Alice thought — what a pity! Jenny would have valued them so much more, from you!

"Don't bother with a lot of cooking, Alice. I had a big lunch. A bit of bread and cheese. And I have a lot of work."

"I'll bring it through to you, if you'd rather."

A trifle too eager. Plainly Alice was no more desirous of spending the ordinary, comfortable domestic evening — a meal in the pretty dining space in the kitchen, a session by the fire — than he was to spend it with her. She had lied to him; he was practically one hundred per cent certain of that; Jenny had confessed to one lie and had possibly told others — about hating Upworth at first sight.

"Through" meant his own room.

"That would suit me fine, if it isn't too much bother. And Alice, I could do with the whisky."

The bother with a wheel-chair was that one could not easily carry things. Hands busy with the propelling, knees with no grip. He could wedge his brief-case, a book, papers beside him, and that was about all.

Alice, willing and efficient — the good nurse — brought the tray. Tom was at his desk, staring with unseeing eyes at some papers.

She said, "Don't overdo it, Tom."

He gave his desk light a little tilt and by its concentrated light, studied her face. She was nearing forty, but a placid, happy nature and splendid health had kept her young-looking; now it was as though the mask had slipped a little. When he said, "Alice," nervousness flickered. He knew what she expected, and hastened to re-assure her. "I've seen that young lout and he's not at all the type. Very spruce, nice manners. I doubt whether a charge would stick. I've decided against bringing one."

"I am so glad." The tension around her mouth and eyes eased a little.

Tom thought — I am also a liar, of a kind. *The charge I bring will stick!*

Thursday, January 25th

"I'm not denying it would be a good thing, Tom dear. But how could *I* go? How would *you* manage?"

"Very well. With some little aid from Mrs Stamper."

Mrs Stamper lived in Overby, but was well-known within a radius of ten miles. She did not work for anybody; she obliged people. She was kindly, competent, reliable and versatile. Correctly approached — and given due notice, she would baby-sit, cook and serve a first-class dinner, nurse the sick, go errands in her small car. She had twice obliged the Penfold family: for a week when Alice caught chicken-pox from Jenny and for three days when Alice had sprained her ankle.

"Have you *asked* her?"

"I have made what are called tentative approaches. She professed herself willing to help out."

"Darling, that might mean anything. She's so busy. She couldn't look after you properly."

"Do I need looking after?"

Not really a very nice question; it diminished Alice in her own esteem. She said,

"Well, to you it may not seem much . . . But I've always had your breakfast ready; and a meal at night.

I've washed. Made your bed. Kept the place clean and tidy . . . If that isn't looking after, you tell me what is."

"Dear Alice! Don't sound so offended. I shall miss you both dreadfully. But I can make my breakfast. And Mrs Stamper proposed coming in on Saturday, making me a meal, taking away anything to be washed. Looking in again on Tuesday, and Thursday. I assure you, I could manage. And the cruise would do you a world of good. You haven't had a proper holiday since you went to the Dutch bulb fields with your Flower Club."

That was true. A lot of old people, infirm people, did go jaunting about, being helped, being pushed. Tom had never, since the verdict, ventured anywhere outside the Works, and this house. He had somehow managed to organise the setting up of the one and the conversion of the other from the shelter of a Nursing Home where the disabled were catered for, and where, as he said, everybody was too busy being sorry for themselves to feel sorry for him. He had a pathological dread of pity. Everybody at the Works knew that the quickest way to get the Boss's goat was to offer a little help with that purring chair if it ran into an awkward position. "Hands off Bolton. I got into this, I'll get out." An innocent young sales representative once opened a clinching argument with the words, "Handicapped as you are, Mr Penfold . . ." and was stopped by Tom's glare. "Handicapped as I am," Tom echoed, furiously. "I'm not in the market for rubbish! Good morning."

He carried this attitude into every walk of life. As he grew prosperous he attracted some attention. A reporter from the *Chesford Advertiser* planned an

44

article to be called "To Success In A Wheel-chair." Tom refused to collaborate: "I don't suppose I can prevent you writing about the business. But if you refer to me as a cripple, I shall sue you. Bad for my image." An empty threat, but it worked. On another occasion he was pressed to appear on a TV programme dealing with physical handicaps and how to overcome them. "It would be such an encouragement to so many people, Mr Penfold." "People who'd be encouraged by staring at me aren't worth encouraging," Tom said harshly. Yet he was a generous and charitable man in the ordinary way.

Now, assuming Alice's consent, he said, "You'll need clothes." He riffled through the gaily coloured travel brochures. "The *Island Queen* sails from Southampton on the 2nd, that's a Friday. I'd suggest that you go up to London on Tuesday, raid the shops for a couple of days, see a play or two, and down to Southampton on Friday morning. I'll lay on hired cars at both ends."

"It's going to be dreadfully expensive . . ."

"Cheaper than a nervous breakdown. Besides, look what we've saved over the years. No holidays. No golf." Poor Tom he had loved his golf! "Most families placed as we are would have had a second car. If Jenny had shown any aptitude, there'd have been a pony, then a horse. We've lived pretty meagrely, Alice; we can afford to splash out for once."

All sound arguments, the most potent the mention of nervous breakdown.

They'd had a wretched week, for something was wrong with Jenny. Hitherto that delicate languishing air

45

had been deceptive; she'd always eaten like a horse. She had a sharp eye for the ridiculous, a gift for mimicry that had enlivened many a meal. Those things that she could do with Tom — *The Times* crossword, playing Scrabble — she had always done with avidity, with increasing expertise. Suddenly all gone. It was a limp, pale, apathetic stranger who emerged. Tom had insisted upon a visit from Dr Shaw who, if old-fashioned, was confident. He did not need a blood test and a report from the pathological department at the Hospital to tell him whether a girl was anaemic or not, he simply pulled down an eyelid and judged by its colour. By this simple test, Jenny Penfold was not anaemic. Despite his archaism the old man was, however, no fool. He agreed absolutely with an opinion once expressed by Doris that growth, both ways, must be allowed for, that all these O-Levels and A-Levels imposed an undue strain upon girls, just at the time when their minds and bodies were facing other demands. Miss Beale and Miss Buss, energetically, and successfully launching girls into the educational stream, had, he thought made a grave mistake, regarding girls as boys, insisting upon parity, ignoring the differences that nature itself imposed. He was himself a father, a grandfather, and he had made observations. During infancy boys were infinitely more vulnerable and up to the age of eleven, more seemingly backward. After that they charged ahead, a tougher growth altogether, as they were designed to be.

He gave his opinion that, for one thing, Jenny had outgrown her strength, shooting up about four inches in a year; and secondly that she had been working too hard. Let her slack off a bit, let the A-Levels wait. There were, after all, nerves to be considered . . .

And not only Jenny's! Alice thought. After all she had nerves, too, and they quivered whenever Tom and Jenny were in the same room. The policy of ignoring the dreadful thing was working so far as actual speech went, but Alice often caught Tom eyeing Jenny in an unfamiliar way; and often when he said, "Jenny . . ." as a prelude to some innocent remark the girl would jump and look positively furtive. A brief separation would be good for everybody.

"Well, Tom if you are sure you can manage, and if Mrs Stamper has promised . . . And if you really can afford it. But it doesn't leave much time. What about booking passages?"

"Dear Alice," he said, pleased with her for not putting up more resistance, "business has all sorts of ramifications. I could get accommodation on any vessel on the Towler-Baker line, even if it meant chucking somebody else overboard. I'll get cracking tomorrow."

And all his arrangements would be perfect, Alice thought fondly. He loved being in control, loved doing anything which went to prove that legs were not a necessity.

"I must get supper, dear. You tell Jenny when she comes down. I bet she'll be thrilled."

Jenny said, "That'll be lovely." Then she went and sat down, opened a book and stared at it.

What was *wrong*? Wouldn't any normal girl — even still suffering from shock — given *carte blanche* to go shopping in London, and then join a cruise, "Out of the English winter to the sunny Caribbean in this luxury floating hotel," to quote the brochures, have shown some sign of pleasure, excitement, interest? No rational parent expected gratitude. The young hadn't asked to be born. They were here because their parents had indulged in some sexual activity motivated by pleasure, duty, habit or drunkeness. All parents, having inflicted "the wound of living" on their offspring, should make every possible compensation.

Nevertheless, there was something puzzling here, and after watching Jenny for ten minutes, during which she did not turn a page, Tom ventured on to ground which, if not explicitly, taboo had tacitly been avoided. On that first evening he had just considered the possibility, young Upworth's appearance and manner had made it seem more feasible, Jenny's behaviour made it almost likely.

He said, "Honey, what with one thing and another we never did have a real heart-to-heart about this . . ."

She looked up, eyes flickering like a nervous horse's.

He blundered on. "Were you by any chance in love with that boy?"

"I told you. I loathed him on sight. You know how I feel about t-o-a-d-s."

He did indeed. Her detestation of the harmless reptile — the gardener's friend — was so intense that she could not bring herself to say the name; and if it occurred, as it did, with rather disproportionate frequency in the crossword puzzles they had once so happily solved together, she'd give up.

"Well, I felt the same about him. From the first. And he *kissed* me! My mouth is better now, but every time I try to eat, or speak, or look in the glass, I feel *sick*. I know it sounds crazy."

Even in this extremity she was Tom's daughter; she gave nothing away. Her mouth, which Dad already knew about; not the rest . . . Not the thing that Dad must never know.

Tom said, "I'm sorry, Honey. But you must *fight* it. It happened, but it's over and done with. You go and have a lovely holiday and forget all about it. Come and look here." He spread out over his immobile knees, the plan of the *Island Queen's* interior. "Double stateroom," he said, pointing to the accommodation he meant to ask for — and get. Then he said a rather cunning thing, "You'll have to look after your mother, Jenny. She is a bit shy of some things. She'd avoid this," he jabbed his finger at the oblong labelled "Jardin du Gourmets," and at the picture which showed a garden, tubbed plants climbing up pillars, up trellises, and a lot of gourmets tucking in to expensive dishes. "You're the travelled one," he said, "and you can read a French menu. You must see that she has a good time. And have a good time yourself. Think honey . . . What he did was abominable. I know. I hold no brief. But *try*. If you must remember, think, every time you do something, or see something nice, he'll be defeated, messing about there in that run-down garage of his."

Her eyes flickered, startled; but all she said was,

"Well, that is one way of looking at it. Thanks, Dad."

Saturday, February 3rd

Half past three in the afternoon; daylight fading. As, in the old days, he had checked vast enterprises, and for the last ten years, smaller ones, Tom checked his arrangements.

He'd had four evenings alone, and although they had been busy ones they had been devoted to comparatively simple things. Manipulating people was less easy. But he'd done it!

The hired car had come for Alice and Jenny at nine o'clock on Tuesday. He had delayed his own departure in order to see them off. At the end Alice had broken down and shed a tear or two and got into the kind of muddle, that had made her a non-driver. She said things like, "Tom, I hate leaving you . . . There're two steaks in the freezer . . . I've left a list for Mrs Stamper . . . On the back seat, please. Jenny have you got everything? The pie only needs heating, darling and don't forget the electricity bill . . ."

In a flurry they'd gone off.

Jack said, "You know, Mr Penfold, if it came to the crunch, Evie'd stand in a bit. She ain't much of a cook, let's face it, but she'd shop. She's a great shopper. You tell me overnight what you want and Evie'll have it there by the time we come past on the way home."

"I will remember that, Jack. Thanks. By the sound of things I'm stocked up for a fortnight at least."

On Wednesday morning, Tom who understood the workings of a combustion engine, said to Jack, who did not, "I don't much like the sound of this."

"Me neither," said Jack, who had noticed nothing. "Take her along to Blake's?"

"Good idea."

"Fill her up at the same time?"

"Sure."

Good, Jack thought; Yellow Stamps still mattered. He and Evie had spent a lot of time, mentally shopping with the Yellow Stamps which the gift of the Kitchen Boy had set free. Anything Mike had, Peter must have — a bare three months between them; and the same with Dolores and Marylin.

The Yeoman, her fault amended, her petrol tank full, ran home like a dream. But on Thursday morning Jack had difficulty in starting her. "Condensation, I'd say, Mr Penfold," he said, using one of the few terms he knew. But he was, Tom thought, sitting in his chair and hearing the futile roar, and then seeing how Jack backed out, downwards, towards the gate, rammed the clutch in, set the engine going and turned, the hell of a good driver.

"I'd say the battery's gone. Keep her going, Jack. Drop me and then come back to Corder's."

51

Baiting the trap.

"Corder's? Excuse me, Mr Penfold, but there didn't look to be much stock there. I doubt whether he'd hev what we need."

"If he's any good he'll get it. I started on a shoe-string, Jack."

True enough.

And then on Friday morning, despite the job which Blake's had done on Wednesday and the new battery which Corder's had supplied and fitted on Thursday, the old girl was on the knock again.

"Now we'll see what Corder's can do," Tom said.

A bit later, with the arrangements made, Jack said, "You know, Mr Penfold, there was no need for all that. I'd have hopped a bus and brought her home for you. Any time tomorrow."

"I know. But by the time you've got me home, and the car back to Corder's, and hopped the bus home, you'll have done your bit, Jack."

"I don't need no bus, come to think of it. I'll just chuck my old bike in the boot and then ride home. Downhill all the way . . . And mark you, if the job is beyond him, or he let you down, you just let me know. Mrs Beeson at the King's Head'd give me a message any time. I could go in early morning and fetch the car."

"I hope that won't be necessary, Jack." An understatement, if ever there was one.

It had seemed logical enough that he — facing a weekend when he must do for himself, should have his electric chair brought home. It took two men to heave it into the boot where it perched, looking like some Heath Robinson device. When they arrived at the house, Tom said, "Now, you're not to touch it, Jack, until I'm ready to help you."

"I can lift it alone."

"You'll do no such thing! One learned gentleman expressed his belief that I am as I am because of an injury I did myself, holding up an iron girder for three minutes."

So far as he favoured any theory, Tom favoured this one. It was certainly preferable to that of functional impairment whose holder had said that he felt it only right to warn Tom that his condition might be progressive. Also, that three-minute struggle with the girder had saved five African lives, and that made the affliction seem less futile.

He installed himself in his wheel-chair and took charge of operations; "Tip it towards me, Jack, till I've got half the weight, then come round and take yours." Ten years of working the wheel-chair at home and heaving himself about on various steel bars, had made him very strong in the arms and shoulders. The electric chair was righted without mishap, but with his usual caution Tom transferred himself to it, and tested it in case it had suffered from the move.

Doris, sent out to buy certain articles of food had made a noble offer. "It'd be no trouble at all for me to come out on the bus on Saturday morning, Mr Penfold and cook you a lunch. And tidy up a bit." This was noble because Doris was a most fanatical supporter of the

Chesford football team — was in fact regarded as their mascot. And this Saturday they were playing away.

"I take that very kindly, Doris, but I'm not averse to a bit of cooking myself. As for tidying; a local woman came in yesterday and left me so spick and span that I'm afraid to knock out my pipe."

"Is she going in regularly while you're alone."

"She'll come whenever I want her."

And that would not be on Saturday!

Mrs Stamper, telephoned by Tom on Friday evening, had not been pleased. The cancelling of engagements was *her* prerogative.

"But, Mr Penfold, I have Saturday morning booked for you."

"I know; but as I say, I've altered my plans. Naturally I'll pay just as though . . ."

"It is not the question of payment." As indeed it was not, she had only to lift the telephone and bring joy to some other house. "It's a question of upsetting my routine." Her sense of outrage, her wish to rebuke came through very strongly.

Unrebuked, Tom said, "My plans are in a state of flux, Mrs Stamper. Perhaps we had better cancel the regular visits. May I ring when I need you?"

You may; but you won't get me!

"That might be best," she said.

The car turned into the short drive, came past the little wild piece of garden where Alice's snowdrops were already white, past the side of the house and into the garage. Seated just inside the kitchen door, Tom was aware of a quickening heartbeat, a shortening of breath. This was how men felt before going into action. Even the element of fear was not lacking. Physical danger was minimal, all other risks were enormous; and the outcome uncertain. What was certain was that he, Thomas Penfold, hitherto a law-abiding citizen, would within a couple of minutes, have committed a crime; one which in a fairly stable democracy must be regarded seriously — taking the law into his own hands.

At the time when the house was being converted, there had still been some slight hope of Alice mastering the art of car-driving. She had tried and failed, but now, with Tom completely helpless, she had a genuine, emotion-backed reason for trying again. With her convenience — should she succeed — in view, Tom had the garage door made very easy to manage. A sliding door that ran back and forth at a touch.

Terry Upworth drove in, got out of the car, gave the door a careless bang and stepped out into the fading light. The old cripple — that was how he always thought of Tom, though he knew his name — had said that he might not be around, so just run the car in and shut the garage door.

Terry did not like Tom — not that that meant much, he disliked most people. But even when Tom was being a potentially good customer, his manner was nasty. Abrupt.

He took hold of the handle; the door ran a little way and then . . . Christ!

Terry knew what had happened, because once, when he was about ten, living in a terraced house in Chesford, their nearest neighbour, an old woman, and old-fashioned enough still to have a wire linen line had been similarly transfixed and immobilised because an electric cable had shifted in a high wind and made her line live. Her husband had heard her shouts and come out, taken her free hand, tried to pull her free and been caught himself; so had another neighbour. Very funny, as good as a circus.

It had taken Terry's father to see what was wrong and lift the cable away with the wooden line-prop.

When it happened to you it wasn't so funny. Especially out here in this bloody wilderness!

He found that he could shout, and he shouted — the old, instinctive human cry. "Help! Help!"

And help was forthcoming. The cripple in his chair.

"Don't touch me, or you'll be stuck too. This handle's gone live."

"I wouldn't willingly touch you with a bargepole," Tom said. "Just stand quite still. I know what to do."

There was a smell, vaguely unpleasant, and then nothing.

He woke in a very strange place indeed. In the ceiling a strip of neon lighting, momentarily blinding to eyes just opened. He was lying on his back on a cold, tiled floor; tiled walls closed him in. Something of the smell persisted. Hospital! I've had a crash! Crashed, but not much hurt. No pain. Left arm. Splint. No. Incredibly his left wrist wore a handcuff, attached by a length of stout chain to a steel bar which came in a right angle out of the wall and into the floor between a washbowl and a lavatory basin.

A police cell.

Well, they might have stolen a march on him, but for once they'd been too clever. Using a handcuff! Dawson would soon see to that.

He reared himself up and shouted. And when shouting brought no response, took off a shoe and hammered, on the floor, on the wall, on any pipe within reach.

They'll pay for this, bleeding bastards!

Nothing happened, nobody came. A more careful and anxious inspection of the place in which he was confined hinted at soundproofing. There was a window shape, completely blocked in with thick white polythene foam; the inside of the door was similarly lined.

For Tom the window had been comparatively easy, all the windows in this house being set low, since as he said, he didn't want to have somebody opening and shutting windows for him. The door had been more of a problem; its upper half well above his head and out of reach. But he'd managed it; almost anything was possible, given time and patience, and the right tools. Three times the topmost of the three panels, thickly smeared with the most powerful adhesive and propelled upwards without any pressure, had failed to stick, and had fallen back on him; but each failure had left some adhesive on the door itself, and at the fourth attempt he had succeeded in holding it there just long enough for the tackiness to take. The second panel had been fairly easy, the bottom one no trouble at all. He had tested the firmness, slamming the door several times. Tested the value of this amateur soundproofing by placing Alice's radio inside the place — the ordinary downstairs cloakroom of a well-planned house. Some sound did emerge, but muted. How much noise the boy would make was, of course incalculable, but as a precaution — not that he expected anyone to call — Tom finally placed the radio on the hall table, opposite the flowerstand, just between the doors of the living-room and the kitchen. He adjusted the control to tune in on what he thought would be the noisiest programme, and left it so that with a flick of the finger, sound of some kind would fill the house.

Terry's watch, the best a doting mother could buy, told the date as well as the time; it informed him that this was still the 3rd, the time four o'clock; half past; five. A year later, six. Shouting, even screaming and the banging had brought no responses and presently a closer examination of his place of confinement convinced him that this was not, after all, a police cell. Some of the tiles were pretty, flowers and birds; the soap on the wash-basin was pink and scented; the towels on the rail, just within reach, pink and fluffy.

So where could he be?

The last clear memory he had was of trying to shut that garage door; of the cripple saying something offensive. Then the blackout. Work back from there. The hospital smell. Hospitals; doctors. Anders! That was as near as he could get. He had enemies, granted; in fact with a few exceptions all men were enemies, but they were scared of him, and they weren't the type to go in for matching soap and towels. It could only be Anders. He'd used some medical trick; anaesthetic on a dart, shot from some hiding place. Terry had seen such a device on TV. Used to catch animals without damaging them.

The idea of being at the mercy of a man like Anders, who had a double grudge, moved his bowels. Common expression enough, "Scare the shit out of him." It was the first time it had happened to him. Lucky the loo was so near.

No good getting in a panic. Use your head!

He knew where Anders lived. In an Upworth house, in an Upworth development in a suburb of Chesford known as Hatch End. Land on that side of the town was scarce and expensive and the Old Man had, as usual, done a bit of cramming; there was very little space between the houses. If he made noise enough . . . And what about Mrs Anders and all those buck-toothed girls? Wouldn't they ask a question or two?

He hammered again and shouted. He took the lid off the cistern and banged it on the floor, and against the wall, cracking several tiles. Somebody *must* hear. Nobody appeared to. Finally he hurled the lid at the window. It fell just short and lay out of reach.

Tom said in what he hoped was a conniving voice, "Is that Chesford 2680?" A girl's voice — surprisingly and hurtfully like Jenny's — said, "Yes. What is it?"

59

"I have a message. Can't say too much on the 'phone. Terry's going to be out of circulation for a bit."

With too ready an understanding the girl said, "Oh! Yes, I see. Thanks for getting in touch."

That was another hurdle successfully negotiated. One weak place patched over. When Tom had said, "Do you do repairs?" the boy had mentioned somebody, a trained man, who worked for him. This person had probably seen, even worked on the car, readily recognisable by its bar. Therefore, Tom reasoned, when young Upworth did not turn up from delivering the car, there would be a clue to his whereabouts. He chose the phrase "out of circulation" because it sounded secretive and vague. It was one of the wildest shots ever launched into the dark, but it seemed to have worked.

Terry reverted to thought.

There was only one person who knew about the cripple's car. A casual glance on Friday evening had shown him that there was no need to call upon Greg; it was a job he could do himself. He'd been doing it on Saturday morning when Nancy arrived, laden with stuff for the blow out and love in planned for the evening. Some of it she'd bought, but most came from her grandmother's deep freeze.

Nancy had set down her baskets and talked for a bit; and she had noticed the steel bar. He knew because she had remarked upon it. "What's that for?" He'd explained, as briefly as possible. He never encouraged Nancy; she was Greg's girl, and all the evidence, not only in stories and films, in real life, went to show that many a good gang had split over the possession of some bitch. He had said, "I'm taking it back this afternoon. If I'm not back by half past four, you know where I leave the key."

Nancy was pretty smart, she'd put two and two together and when he didn't turn up, she'd tell Greg and Peter where to *begin* to look. There was a gap which even he himself couldn't bridge. The gap between the garage door and this place, wherever this was . . .

Thinking of Nancy — no mean cook, her ultimate aim had once been the Cordon Bleu, and what at this moment was being prepared in the rather dark little kitchen — made him temporarily aware of hunger. He'd always eaten well; even in the old days when his Old Man had been struggling. Mum was no fancy cook, but she believed in food and produced good solid meals, often with some little extra for Terry on the sly, because he was growing. It was in fact, Mum's belief in food that had defeated the Old Man's plan to keep Terry at Crosfield. What was the good of a fancy education, she demanded, if you had to starve to get it? Her word carried weight; she kept the firm's books!

Her son, held captive, kidnapped, completely emptied out, had no recourse but to drink water.

The door bell chimed.

Who the devil? Passing the radio, Tom flicked it and it instantly obliged with a programme called "Happy Families." Very noisy.

He opened the door, saw Josh Salter and his dog, had no time even to say hullo before the dog pushed in, hackles up, teeth bared, straight for the cloakroom door.

"Excuse *us*," Josh said, pushing past almost as unceremoniously. He took Gyp by the scruff of her neck and hauled her into the sitting-room. "You daft old baggage," he said, in a tone as nearly un-doting as Tom had ever heard him use towards her.

"Well. Evening, Mr Penfold. I thought I'd look in, hearing you was all on your own."

"Very neighbourly. Have a drink." Unwelcome as they were at the moment one must remember the debt of gratitude. But for this man and this dog . . .

"We been away for a bit. Cheers."

"Cheers. Yes, so I noticed." He noticed, too that both man and dog, never well-fleshed, had lost weight.

"Had a horrible time. All on account of *her*. Wouldn't eat, wouldn't settle. Couldn't sleep, nor let me. Tell you a joke, Mr Penfold. I was so concerned in the end I got a vet to her. Very suspicious, he was, said she was pining, asked me how long I'd had her. See? Thought I'd pinched her. How's that?"

"Very comic."

Because his ear was attuned and informed, Tom could hear the noise young Upworth was making. But it blended exactly with the programme whose title was ironic.

"Still, in a way, he hit the nail on the head. She *was* pining. Homesick. Had to bring her home or she'd have died on me. *Will you come here and lay.*"

He had brought her home in desperation. And there'd been no official communication on his mat. Nothing about a dog out of control, biting for the second time; just a lot of bumph about detergent with a coupon worth 3p, and electoral letters from three people who wanted to get onto the County Council. It had all served to start up the fire.

So Gyp seemed safe enough, that was the main thing. As for the other . . . If Mr Penfold had meant to kick up a fuss, with witnesses, he wouldn't have sent his girl — chief witness of all — off on a holiday. Would he? Still, it would be nice to know.

Tom said, "I've always been led to believe that only cats formed attachments to places rather than persons."

"So I reckoned. I was a bit hurt, tell you the truth. But she's clever. See what I mean? I was the one that took her to a place she didn't much like, so in a way she turned against me. There ain't many dogs as could work that out. *Will you come here and lay.*"

"She does seem rather restless."

"She ain't had her proper run yet. Had to go into the village. Got some meat for us both. That was how I heard. And if there's anything I can do . . . I know gardens don't need much tending just now, but I'm a good hand with a frying pan. Cook you a fry up any time."

"That's a noble offer. I might take you up on it. But not just yet. My wife left me well provided for."

"She would," said Josh who admired Alice without liking her. "All right then, we're on our way." He stood up. The positive reassurance that he had come for, had not been offered. "I take it you let that other matter drop, Mr Penfold."

"Which other matter?"

"Young Upworth . . ."

"What could I do? I bore in mind what you said about his alibi. You, the only witness, had vanished. Jenny didn't want to talk about it even. I dropped it."

"Very wise. Very wise. A young rogue who'd rob his own father . . ."

"Did he?"

"All hushed up of course, but don't tell me Daphne Upworth wouldn't know her own boy, nylon stocking or no nylon stocking. Two masked men, she said. And easy to see why. Upworth was just named for Mayor. The last thing they'd want was dirty linen . . . Now would you believe that . . ."

The lurcher had flung herself at the free swinging door, moved it enough to squeeze through.

"Mad to get home." But she had not made for the front door. She was back at the door of the cloakroom, pawing and pushing; angered because it did not yield so easily.

Once again Josh grabbed her and dragged her away.

"Honestly, anybody'd think that boy had been here."

Now, try out the story for the first time; and be glad that the trial run should be made with a man grappling with a dog.

"Curiously enough, he was. Only this afternoon." This chair was so much more easily manoeuvred. Tom placed it between Gyp and her enemy, edging her and her master towards the door. "He did a job on my car, and brought it back. And went in there to wash up before getting back to the bus."

"You mean you give him a job?"

"There again I had no choice. Blake's cram-jam full. Friday afternoon . . ."

Josh said, "AAAH. Yes, I see." He saw it all. He was himself part of the underworld, but in a minor way; a few poached pheasants and partridges and a little information — the result of seemingly aimless rambles about the countryside — as to which farmer had a nice flock of turkeys, or a batch of bullocks pastured out. His contacts in Leicester offered a ready market for such things. He knew a good deal about the seamier side of life and the workings of bribery, of there always being more in any situation than was immediately visible. He now deduced that what he and Gyp had disturbed had been a bit of rough courting; that Mr Penfold, once he knew, had disapproved, sent the girl off on a long holiday and given young Upworth his custom in exchange for a promise of silence.

That being so, all you could say was that the man was a damn good actor.

"How's his hand? Where Gyp nailed him?"

"Oh, only superficial wounds. He had the plasters off in a week."

"Teeth ain't what they were, I suppose. Gyp, if you don't behave yourself, you'll be back on the lead. Well, goodnight, Mr Penfold. I'll look in from time to time. You shan't be lonely."

"Oh, I shan't be lonely. I'm taking advantage of being alone to catch up on some work."

65

Now for a bit of psychological treatment. Tom pushed the kitchen door to the position in which it stayed open, and prepared his supper — grilled steak and fried onions. The cloakroom was only just across the hall. The flavoursome scent would penetrate.

Torture. That was what it was. Torture of the refined kind that Terry had read about and enjoyed. He was not a great reader but he enjoyed some books, notably those paperbacks published under the sign Double X. They were not exactly pornographic. Thank God he was sexually normal and needed no such stimulation. Double X books were openly on display in Peter's bookshop, alongside Penguins. Pan Books and Corgis. Peter did a brisk trade in the other kind, but you had to know the password in order to get one . . .

Peter was so clever, or supposed to be so clever. Surely by now — ten o'clock — he'd have worked out, from what Nancy had to say, that whatever had happened to Terry had happened at a place called The Old Barn, Dove Lane, Overby. In which case Greg, the strong one and Peter the clever one, would have gone to Overby and somehow picked up the trail. A cripple shouldn't be too hard to handle, and anything the cripple knew, they'd know now.

Terry was almost certain that he had Dr Anders to blame for the situation in which he found himself. The cripple might have connived . . . though why he should — except that such people did always stick together — Terry couldn't see. He'd never done the cripple any harm! Nor would it be true to say that he'd done

Anders any harm, really. His precious son — buck-toothed like his sisters, had joined on his own accord. Free, white, and seventeen ... Admittedly, when Anders was fuming and threatening action, he'd been defeated and silenced by a very cunning move. And was now taking vengeance.

His watch said ten o'clock. There were three positions he could occupy; he could stand up; he could close the lavatory seat and sit; he could lie down on the floor. And the place was growing colder. (Tom's central heating was well-geared; it switched off at nine-thirty, and on again at six in the morning.)

The strip light in the ceiling shed its cold light. One of the Double X stories had dealt with this exact problem — the denial of the sleep-inducing darkness. He was hungry. He'd breakfasted as usual on a boiled egg, and then, in anticipation of Nancy's love feast, lunched lightly, on a hamburger, and now he must sleep, if he could sleep, on the floor. And never in his life had he had any but a comfortable bed. Even after the chuck-out and his precipitate move to the house attached to Corder's, Mum had done her stuff. His good bed, with its Sleep-tite mattress, its down pillows and eiderdown had been there almost as soon as he was.

Now he slept on the floor of hard cold tiles. And not well.

Sunday, February 4th

Tom grilled bacon, frizzling it into a state of inedibility in order to diffuse the scent. With the same end in view he overbrewed the coffee.

Milk was delivered at the back door by a man in a hurry. The Sunday papers thudded in at the front. Apart from that dead silence until Overby church bell issued its slightly cracked summonses to the faithful.

Odd to remember that Mrs Cooper's brave effort last summer had been ambivalent, all the posters and invitations saying OXFAM in capitals — Oxfam being a popular cause, and in small print, a bit shame-facedly, "10 per cent of the proceeds to the restoration of St Matthew's bell."

Equally odd to realise that what he had said, defensively to Salter, proved to be true. He had work to do, and he was still capable of concentrating. When at twenty past twelve the telephone rang, it gave him quite a jerk.

"Mr Penfold . . ." Mrs Cooper's unmistakable voice, loud, masterful. It was somehow typical that although for years she had called Alice and Jenny by their Christian names, she had never ventured so far with him. She'd made the original mistake of thinking that a man with useless legs was malleable. He'd soon put her right on that.

But now she sounded kind and concerned.

"I only just heard — coming out of church. I've been away and didn't get back until yesterday. I know you can't come to lunch, you couldn't squeeze into my mini. I know! I know! But I really have such a lovely saddle of lamb and all the accessories. And one of those excellent, old-fashioned hot water dishes. It would be no trouble to me, absolutely a pleasure, to bring you a nice hot lunch, Mr Penfold."

Meals on Wheels!

"That is very kind of you, Mrs Cooper. But in fact I have my joint in the oven. Thanks all the same."

"Oh." Frustrated in her do-gooding. Deflated. "I didn't realise that you could *cook*. I'm hopeless myself, but I have Margerita, thank God. And Pedro for the garden . . . I have said, more than once that bread cast on the waters bobs up again as buttered toast."

Irritating, because he had heard it before. And how few people had so much bread to cast? Empty lodges, furnished cottages.

"It is very kind of you, Mrs Cooper; but please don't bother about me. I can look after myself."

"Yes . . . Alice always said that you were very independent."

"Alice, as usual was right."

And yet, if Jenny was to be believed, Alice and Mrs Cooper had both been dead wrong. Mrs Cooper had, actually started the whole thing, saying that the young

69

must be attracted, and who nowadays, wanted to bowl for a pig? And Alice had coaxed Jenny into going . . . Be sociable, be helpful. On the other hand, perhaps it was wrong to blame the Oxfam do. Kate Dawson was somehow mixed up in this.

His anxiety to know the truth, to get to the bottom of things almost made him impatient; but he'd wait the twenty-four hours which he had decided upon. Twenty-four hours of solitary confinement, with no food, should bring the boy to his senses.

Terry was by this time certain that wherever he was, it was not Dr Anders' House at Hatch End. Too quiet. The place was not fully sound-proofed; he'd heard the doorbell, a brief spell of noise from a radio or TV. The telephone. But no traffic. Hatch End on a Sunday was full of cars because of the golf course. So he did not know where he was; and nor did anybody else. Somebody — probably Anders — had got the better of him, kidnapped him and left him to die. Why? For what?

He went through one of the mad fits which had long ago gained him his change of name from Terry to Terror. He lunged against the chain and did nothing but hurt himself, for the handcuff fitted tightly, and the steel bar had been designed to withstand more weight than he could produce. Somebody meant to starve him to death. He screamed and there was no answer. Frenzy gave way to self-pity and despair. Why should anybody wish to starve him to death? He'd never done anybody much harm. And even if he had . . . Even the Moors Murderers were fed, given proper beds.

Julia Walpole had drowned herself, but she'd done that on her own accord, just as she'd done everything that led up to the act. Mrs Walpole had blamed him, but she was daft as a coot, and had ended in an asylum.

Asylum! His thoughts shifted. Maybe the only place where they dare handcuff people and chain them to the wall nowadays, would be a lunatic asylum. Had he, in one of his ungovernable rages, gone a little too far. Blacked out with rage, in fact.

He had felt angry when that bleeding cripple — to whom he'd done a favour — made that contemptuous, uncalled for remark. Maybe that, combined with a slight electric shock, had sent him temporarily round the bend. And Penfold, of course, was just the kind who would rush straight to the telephone and report that he had a madman on his hands.

Wait a minute; weren't there formalities before even a raving lunatic could be committed? A doctor; or even two? Anders would do it with the utmost joy, and could easily find another doctor to agree. But there was the time. When he blacked out it had been his intention to catch the four o'clock bus at Overby King's Head. When he came round, in this place, his watch said four o'clock; so he couldn't have been out for more than fifteen minutes, so how? There was an answer — the watch had been affected by that slight flow of electric current. And was no longer to be relied upon. So now, in addition to being unsure of his whereabouts, he didn't even know the time, or the date.

And if, by some chance he *had* landed in a madhouse, his behaviour hadn't helped. Shouting and banging. Maybe the reason nobody had come near was because nobody dared. He'd be very quiet from now on. And when, at last, somebody did come, calm, cool and collected, he'd soon talk his way out of this. And once he was out somebody was going to be very, very sorry.

Even now he did not doubt his ability to talk his way out. It had always served him — with one remarkable exception, his final row with his father, and even then tonguemanship had saved him from the worst.

A glib tongue had saved him from the shame of expulsion from Broadfield, that hated place, where for the first time in his life he had been disciplined and made to conform, more or less. The Head had actually said — "Upworth, your behaviour can no longer be tolerated. I feel — most reluctantly — obliged to ask your father to withdraw you, at the end of this term."

Terry had got his word in first; with his mother. The food was awful; the water was never hot; and everybody had it in for him because he'd complained. They were cooking up some kind of tale about his bad behaviour, but that was simply an excuse. Mum had acted. Terry had left — he had not been expelled. He had finished his education at the local Grammar School. There he had been just as troublesome as he had been at Broadfield; but even when, in sheer desperation, a master had sent him to the Headmaster's study, nothing happened. This Head, in addition to living in an Upworth house, with a heavy mortgage, was a

72

Mason, a Rotarian, a member of the Golf Club Committee, spheres in which Upworth senior held power. Rebukes in the Head's study took the form of soft-soaping. Upworth enjoyed advantages, denied to some, a good home, good parents, why not try to do them credit? Upworth had brains, why not use them? Why not set a good example?

Just talk. And every time he could match it, outwit it.

Planning now to talk himself out — if indeed this were an asylum — he made a last, desperate attempt to retrieve the cistern lid. Throwing it had been the act of a lunatic. He failed to reach it because the downstairs cloakroom at The Old Barn had been big enough to allow Tom to enter it, use it, turn his chair around. For Tom's convenience too, this bar had been fixed. He had his own bathroom, but it was at some distance along the hall. For trivial extra expense, the downstairs cloakroom, readily accessible from the kitchen, from the garden, had been planned and fitted.

Sunday afternoon silence settled down. In his makeshift cell Terry toyed with the idea of declaring himself to be an epileptic. Epileptics could get away with murder. When that door opened — as surely it must, soon — he had his tale ready.

His watch — no longer to be relied upon — indicated that the time was four o'clock, the date the 4th, when the door did open, revealing exactly what Terry had seen just before he blacked out; that crippled bastard in his chair.

Skip the police, skip Anders, skip the lunatic asylum; something else; something for which he was entirely

73

unprepared. He'd blacked out with this bugger looking at him and now, after what seemed a lifetime, here they were, facing one another again.

Tom spoke first.

"Before I come within arm's reach of you, I should warn you. You and I are alone here; and nobody knows where you are. If you injure me, you'll starve."

"Why would I want to injure you, Mr Penfold?" Once again Terry's mind shifted quickly. The man had gone mad! Wasn't there a saying about cripples always feeling that the world owed them a limb? Drugs too, easing pain, sending people daft. It wasn't Terry Upworth who'd gone dotty outside that garage door, it was this bloody . . .

"It would be natural for you to resent this treatment."

"Well," Terry said, drawing the word out in an inconclusive way, making it sound as though there were nothing *so* extraordinary in the situation. The mad must be humoured. He assumed his most engaging manner. "Turn me loose, Mr Penfold, and we'll say no more about it. I shan't bear a grudge. I shan't even mention it." It sounded like a bargain. Terry had been reared on them, believed in them. People looking over a not-quite-completed house and being dubious about a north aspect, a lack of view or a cramped kitchen could almost always be wooed over by being promised their own choice of colour when it came to decorating. The Upworth colours were so enticingly named; never pink, Orchid.

The madman proved to be insusceptible to cajolery or bargaining. He gave positive proof of lunacy by saying,

"You are being punished. You will stay where you are until you are *genuinely* sorry for what you did to my daughter."

The expression on the boy's face could have been simple astonishment.

"What *I* did? To your daughter? Mr Penfold I didn't even know you had one."

"Maintain that attitude and you will be here a long, long time."

This door naturally had a catch; Tom could not back out; he was obliged to manoeuvre his chair about and reach for the handle. That gave Terry time to recover.

"Wait! I swear. It's God's truth. I don't know what happened to your daughter, but it wasn't me. You've got the wrong man. I never set eyes on your daughter. I didn't know she existed."

"Can you deny that on January 18th you assaulted a girl, just along this lane?"

It was more than a fortnight since he'd taught that snooty bitch a lesson; snub after snub avenged there in the mud. He'd got her out of his system and had almost forgotten. He'd never expected to hear any more about it; she wasn't the sort to go wailing in to her mother. Too proud! And if she had and they'd wanted to make something of it, he'd got his alibi all right. And if they wouldn't accept that, something to say that would make them regret ever having let out a squeak.

"I did *meet* a girl, somewhere near here, not long ago," he said cautiously. "But it wasn't your daughter. It was Jenny Cooper."

"It was my daughter, Jenny Penfold. And you didn't meet her. You assaulted her."

"Then why go about calling herself Cooper?" That really puzzled him. As for assaulting. He had, all ready, that something to say that which, in the last resort, would have made the Coopers look silly. "You can't call it assault, when the girl's ready and willing."

Tom felt sickened, partly by his own lack of surprise. Hadn't he, from the very first, sensed something odd in the way Jenny had behaved? Something secret; a lack of candour.

"I'd better hear your version," he said, falling into the error many other men had committed. Upworth, let's hear what you have to say. Upworth had always had plenty to say, and more often than not it had been effective.

Terry felt bold enough to ask for something to eat. Tom handed over the slice of bread which he had brought. It was rather stale. He didn't eat much bread or any other form of carbohydrate because he had a dread of getting heavy, less able to heave himself about.

The boy took the slice and wolfed it. And he reverted to practical thought. Ever since he had hit on the idea that he might be in an asylum, and begun to distrust his watch, he hadn't been sure of place, time, or date.

He said, almost conversationally, "I've lost count of time in here."

"It is Sunday, February 4th. The time is ten minutes past four."

There was still hope then, even if he failed to talk his way out. It might take Nancy a bit of time to put two and two together; time for Peter to plan something, for Greg and Jerry to put the plan into execution. He knew now where he was; the cripple had said, "We are alone here," and that could only mean the Old Barn, Dove Lane, Overby. And to that place, Nancy surely could point the way. Meanwhile, even if he hadn't talked his way out by the time the gang arrived, he'd give this bleeding cripple something to think about. Using the word *punished*. To Terry Upworth! Who set him up as a judge?

"It was like this," Terry began. The beauty of it was that quite a bit of what he had to tell was true; always a help. "Back last summer, just up the lane here there was a charity do and Eddie Lane and his group were hired to play. So some of us came to support him. And I danced with . . . There was something about her. Put me through the mangle and I couldn't name it, really . . ." Dead right, he'd never been able to explain, even to himself. He'd always favoured brunettes, plump, bouncy, forthcoming. Why he should go and fall for a pale, unfriendly . . . "Kind of romantic. Pre-Raphaelite."

The word sounded strange here, in this narrow cell. But it was apt. Terry Upworth had picked his way through all that education, private and expensive, public and free, had offered. A magpie, snatching up

77

what was attractive, hating anything that demanded effort.

"Maybe it was the hair . . . Anyway, I offered to run her home on the back of my bike, and she said she was at home. So later I asked Eddie who'd hired him and he said Mrs Cooper. Oh, and I had told her my name, and she'd said hers was Jenny. So, you see? Jenny Cooper."

A natural enough mistake. And so far this account tallied exactly with Jenny's.

"Go on," Tom said. Terry did not immediately resume. He had just realised how Kate Dawson and Colin Anders had fooled him. Even when it was *his* party. On his best behaviour he'd said, "Miss Cooper," and they hadn't corrected him. They'd probably had a giggle about it, behind his back. At the thought anger glowed red in his light-brown eyes. He was obliged to admonish himself — Keep cool. And strike to wound.

"The point was, I could tell by her look that she liked me, too and would have liked . . . if she hadn't had to go into the house to help her mother, as I thought. So a night or two later I ran out and went up to the house. It was more or less shut up and there was nobody about except some Wops and all I could make out from them was that the family was away."

Again correct. Having done her bit for Oxfam and the church bell, Mrs Cooper had gone to Peru to visit her daughter and see her latest grandchild.

"A fortnight, or maybe three weeks later, I looked in again. Wops, as before. And a very savage dog on the prowl." He managed a little self-deprecating laugh.

"Not to mention a visit next day from the police. One of the Wops was nervous; he'd taken my number and said he thought I was casing the joint. I ask you!"

(Peter once, in a sour mood, had pointed out to Terry that some of his expressions gave him away. Peter was pedantic; he was down on the prevalent "You know." "Terry, if I knew I shouldn't be asking.")

Tom said, "And then?"

"I saw her again. Outside the school. I was waiting for somebody else, but that was not important. I ditched it and offered to run her home. And again she said she couldn't, because she was going home to tea with Kate Dawson. But she gave me that look again. So I went about it differently. I knew Colin Anders; I knew he was mad keen on Kate Dawson. I fixed up — arranged — a party. Dinner at that Chinese place — The House of the Seventh Joy. A foursome. Kate, Colin, Jenny and myself. It was a good party, too."

This was something Jenny had not mentioned. Why?

"Good, that is until the end. The two girls disappeared and the Dawson b . . . Kate came back alone. She said Jenny wasn't feeling too good — something she'd eaten, and she'd sent her home in a taxi."

Tom remembered the occasion. But Jenny had said nothing about feeling ill; she said she had missed the bus.

"Next day she sent me a note."

"I don't suppose you have it on you."

The boy had a wallet, Tom knew, because at the end of the slow difficult haul, with the electric chair making heavy work of towing the inert body sprawled on the rug, he had gone through the boy's pockets and removed cigarettes and a lighter. The stuff with which door and window were lined was easily inflammable. He had not opened the wallet.

"As a matter of fact, I have." He produced the wallet — a very superior article, crocodile skin with gold corners. "Nothing very personal," he said, handing Tom a sheet of paper torn from an exercise book.

They taught an Italianate style of writing nowadays, but even through its formality individuality broke through, and this was Jenny's hand. "Dear Mr Upworth, Thank you for a lovely dinner. I'm sorry I had to leave early. Yours sincerely, Jenny."

Nothing very personal, certainly. But why write at all? Such minor courtesies as thank-you letters were out-dated. Tom handed back the paper and Terry stowed it away in a wallet that seemed to contain rather a lot of money. Then he took out a snapshot. It showed Jenny, in a pretty blue frock, standing by a clump of white lilies. The rest of the garden background was unfamiliar and the photograph itself was one that Tom had never seen before. Jenny looked very pretty, very graceful amongst the lilies, very — as the boy had said — pre-Raphaelite. As a rule — and Tom had taken dozens of her, all kept by Alice in an album — she did not photograph as well as loving eyes would have liked.

"It's written on," Terry said. So it was. Jenny's writing again. "Looking human for once !!!!!"

"She gave you this?"

"How else would I have had it?"

It was like walking through a swamp with every step plunging one in more deeply. Handing it back, Tom said,

"We're still quite a long way from what happened in the lane."

"Well, as I said, I liked her, and knew she liked me, but it wasn't easy to meet. Kate and Colin said her mother — I thought it was Mrs Cooper then — was very strict, and I could well believe it; she'd struck me as the masterful sort. I went round to the school a time or two, but I was always unlucky." That, at least fitted with Jenny's story. "Then Colin Anders brought me a message, making a date. The first I couldn't keep, much as I would have liked to, but after all, I have business to see to. It had to be Thursday, just after nine. The only time she was off the hook. The second time was that fog — not that that would have stopped me — but there was that smash-up at the roundabout and all traffic diverted. So I was late. And then, at last we made it. And, as I said, she was ready and willing."

Tom said, handling the words as though they were filthy rags,

"If she was so ready and willing, why did you have to black her eye?"

"If I did it was accidental. I hit out at the dog."

That fitted, in a way. It was like a jig-saw puzzle designed by an idiot, pieces fitting into place but giving no over-all picture. Tom was still trying to work it out when the doorbell chimed. Alice had insisted upon chimes because, as she so sensibly said, when she was at the further end of the garden the sound of an

81

ordinary doorbell and the telephone were practically indistinguishable.

Answering the chime, switching on the porch light, opening the door, Tom expected to see Josh Salter, come for a free drink. With his horrible dog. He'd get short shrift.

But under the harsh light, against a background curtain of sleet, rapidly turning to snow, was Sergeant Bateson, the young, fresh-faced police officer.

"Something has turned up, sir," he said. He held, as though it were a cherished child, a bulky parcel, brown paper and an outer wrapping of polythene.

"Come in," Tom said. Before moving to the door he had switched on the radio which had obliged with a tremendous noise, a full-voiced Welsh choir, singing lustily.

The living-room had the dead, flat, unwanted atmosphere of a room seldom used, of a place which had not really rubbed shoulders with a human being for quite a long time. Alice had always contended that central heating was all very well, but a fire was *company*. No fire now. No bit of knitting or mending; no living thing. Alice's winter stand-by, a thing called a Christmas cactus had been moved out on to the stand in the hall so that it could be watered with the other plants. A truly inhospitable room; and to a police officer on duty one could not even make the hospitable gesture of offering a drink.

"As you were informed, sir, no vagrant was found in this area, though a close watch was maintained. But early this morning, at Stoke St Martin a man was arrested. He had this on him."

With a juggler's move Sergeant Bateson unshrouded his parcel and exposed to view the replica of Jenny's bag.

"Contents as described — even to the five-pound note."

He spoke with a certain quiet triumph. The mills of investigation might grind slowly but they didn't miss much. It seemed rather a shame to say, as Tom was bound to,

"It does resemble my daughter's, but it is not hers."

Tom knew what had happened to Jenny's bag, to everything else associated with that horrible evening. Alice had had a bonfire.

Identification mattered, for the fiver was one of the forged ones which had been bedevilling the district; and there was more hope of tracing it through a responsible citizen like Mr Penfold than through a thief and a meth-drinker.

"I think, perhaps," Sergeant Bateson suggested respectfully, "the young lady . . ."

"She's away. But you can take my word. It's like hers, but it is not the same. I know. I bought hers. As you can imagine, I don't do much shopping. What I do, I remember."

"Yes, I suppose you would . . ." Without meaning to do so, the young, strong man glanced at the useless legs. Tom thought — I wonder what you would say, how you would look, if you knew that I had something worse than a thief in custody, as you'd call it; that I took him single-handed.

"Funny though. Everything just as described." It could have been accident, or design, but his big, cold-reddened hands worked the catch on the bag's flap and the odour of stale, heavily sensuous scent crept out. Faintly unclean.

"Don't tell me," Tom said quickly. "My daughter is very fair; she uses a compact powder called . . . called White Rose."

Dutifully Sergeant Bateson examined the compact he held. Apricot Glow.

"When she uses lipstick it is Blush Rose." The one in the bag was Persian Poppy. Also, now that he came to look closely, Sergeant Bateson saw that the comb, which was dirty, had some black hairs tangled in its teeth. The odour of scent and of uncleanliness was concentrated in a grubby handkerchief with some smears of lipstick on it.

"I'm sorry to have bothered you sir," he said. "But it is quite a coincidence, isn't it?"

"It's a chain-store bag, this season's fashion. And fivers aren't all that rare nowadays."

Sergeant Bateson repacked the bag carefully and remarked that it was setting in for a nasty night.

In the hall he said, "Very musical, the Welsh." The set needed adjustment, he thought, for there was interference from another programme; somebody shouting.

Terry had heard, first the chiming doorbell, then the radio. Rescue was at hand. Naturally the cripple would say that he'd left in the ordinary way, yesterday afternoon. And of course Greg and Peter would believe him, because the truth was so incredible. That was an aspect of the situation which had not struck him before.

He shouted, calling Greg, Peter, Jerry by name, calling, "I'm here."

Nothing happened. Presently the radio was silenced. Terry waited for the door to open. But it did not.

He looked back over his story, and thought it held up very well. By rights the cripple bastard should be here, turning him loose, apologising. For on the face of it, what had he done? Tumbled a willing girl who'd made a date with him. Even the black eye satisfactorily explained. So why wasn't the bastard here, turning him loose and apologising?

The silence was absolute.

Maybe something had happened; a fit, or a stroke. The old fool was obviously set on his daughter, you could tell that by the way he said, "my daughter", by the way he'd looked at her handwriting and the picture of her, by the action he had taken as a revenge.

Maybe the thought that she'd been playing round had brought on a stroke. Terrible thought. You and I are alone here and nobody knows where you are. Out of circulation . . .

"Appears to be incapable of logical thought," a waspish master had once written on a report form. Sitting on the hard lid of a lavatory seat, chained to a steel bar, Terry Upworth saw suddenly how illogical his hopes of rescue had been. The cunning bleeder had warned them that he wouldn't be around for a bit.

Terry, in fact had not been thinking straight. But even for that he had an excuse ready. He had always been able to excuse himself to himself, as well as to other people. On Saturday afternoon he'd been unconscious for at least half an hour; in twenty-eight hours he'd had nothing but water and a crust of bread. And no cigarettes.

Odd, he hadn't missed them at first — possibly as a result of the anaesthetic; then his craving for food had taken foremost place. Now he wanted a cigarette more than he'd ever wanted anything. Just one.

And he'd always had exactly what he wanted. Mum had seen to that. Take that stupid rule at Broadfield about all cakes being shared. It had been carefully explained; lots of boys there had parents abroad, who couldn't deliver cakes with any regularity; therefore any boy who had a cake must produce it and share it with his whole table. Mum had dealt with that, as she had dealt with sterner problems in her day. She always brought or sent *two*; one for public sharing, which even his Old Man had said he thought was a bit on the Commie side, and one for private consumption.

Another, more kindly report had said, "Does not lack imagination." Nor he did. He had a lively imagination, but it did not function in the direction of putting himself in anybody else's shoes. Even now, craving for a cigarette he did not relate his longing to those of other people, longings he had exploited. Nothing of that kind. At the moment his imagination was concerned with the possibility that Tom Penfold had had another stroke. Also, very vaguely with the idea that if he ever got out of here, he'd take such vengeance on the bloody bastard . . . Nothing short of ruin. To take his mind off it he began to plan it. And felt better.

Tom was at the telephone. In this idiot jig-saw puzzle, where some pieces fitted and some did not, Colin Anders had a place.

At the other end of the line, Dr Anders said, "Yes, speaking." He sounded tired, as he was. It had been his week-end on duty; it was almost six o'clock on a Sunday evening. Felicity was about to play Bridge; Bridge was her refuge from misery and who could grudge it? She'd cooked earlier for the girls, who were now going about whatever girls did busy themselves with. Dr Anders had missed that meal and was looking forward to his supper. A good wedge of veal and ham pie, left under a very clean cloth, alongside the sandwiches with which, presently, the Bridge players were to be refreshed and strengthened. With a cold snack, on a cold evening at the end of a tiresome day, a whisky and soda would have been agreeable, but the brutal fact was that he could not afford whisky just now. He'd make a cup of tea. As he filled the kettle the telephone rang.

"My name is Penfold." It rang a bell, very faintly. A name he *should* know, but couldn't immediately place. "I'd like a word with Colin."

Dr Anders stiffened. The name he almost knew might well be one mentioned in one of those long maudlin sessions.

"That is impossible," he said curtly. "He isn't here."

"When will he be back?" Only God knew the answer to that.

"Not for some considerable . . . What's the name again?"

"Penfold. Tom Penfold. I live at Overby."

Got it! Old Shaw's wonder patient; legs completely useless, guts enough for a dozen.

In a milder voice he said, "Oh yes. Mr Penfold. I'm sorry but my boy is . . . away. I shall probably be seeing him this week." He could for a moment see no possible connection between Colin and the man who ran Component Parts from his wheel-chair, but then everything lately had seemed a bit disconnected. "I could take a message." Take, not necessarily deliver. Then a possible connection suggested itself. Even before things went so wrong, Colin had been unsettled, talked about not wanting to stay at school and clock up the extra necessary A-Levels; not wanting, after all, to be a doctor, wanting to do something more immediately remunerative. (And this was Colin, who, aged six, had gone round the garden on his tricycle, calling upon the delphiniums and roses and dahlias, asking, "And how are you today?" God, the hopes, the ambitions!) He might have approached Penfold and asked for a job. And it was irrefutable that Colin would be better off *here*, under his father's eye. Later on.

"It's a bit difficult," Tom said. "What I wanted was for Colin to corroborate, or refute a statement made to me. It concerns my daughter."

Holy Mother of God! How could the name have meant so little? Colin; Kate Dawson; Jenny Penfold, anaemic looking girl with lovely hair. The three names led inevitably to a fourth; Terry Upworth.

It took Dr Anders so short a time as to be no time at all, to think — Not to recognise the name *Penfold*; I must be *slipping*! And to relate everything to Upworth is *obsessional*. I've got to be a little careful with myself!

His professional manner held, however and much as he would have asked what were the symptoms, he asked, "Does it also concern young Upworth?"

"Almost entirely," Tom said.

And, very much as he would have said if the voice at the other end of the line had reported a double fracture, Dr Anders said, "*Do nothing, Penfold. I'll be right over. Say half an hour.*"

He knew it was snowing, but that cut both ways. No traffic.

"How do I find you?"

"There's the King's Head. The lane opens just opposite. I'm the second house down on the left."

Tom switched on the porch light, and lit the fire in the living-room. From time to time his captive called, "Mr Penfold! Mr Penfold!"

And I may be wrong. Was it Cromwell who had said something to Parliament, beseeching them, by the bowels of Christ to consider that they might be wrong.

89

I may be wrong. The note, the snapshot. Jenny trying to slink upstairs. *She wasn't crying then*, he remembered. She only began to cry when she realised that the secret was no longer secret.

Also, now that he came to think of it, wasn't there something slightly sinister in Dr Anders' reaction. Six o'clock on a snowy Sunday evening — I'll be right over! — just as he would have responded to an emergency call. What did he know?

Dr Anders' profession had accustomed him to entering strange houses with the minimum of fuss. He shook hands with Tom, slipped out of his overcoat, folded it and laid it on the hall chair.

"In here," Tom said, speaking loudly to be heard above the gales of almost frenzied laughter emitted by the radio.

"Nice to see a fire. It's a filthy night." He stretched his freckled hands to the blaze.

"And you may feel that I've dragged you out for nothing."

"Nothing that concerns young Upworth is nothing to me." All the way from Chesford he'd been asking himself — What now? What's come to light that I don't know about?

"Have a drink." Anders turned his head. What an array of bottles!

"Whisky and soda please. Make it weak. I missed my lunch. I was just about to eat when you . . ."

"I'm sorry," Tom said, busy at the table. "And it may well be that you can't help."

"Thanks. There's one way in which I *can* help. At least, I hope so." He took a sip, then another. "What's this about Colin?"

He was still quite a substantial man, but his clothes — especially his collar — had the look of having been made for somebody bigger. His face, freckled like his hands, should have been firm-fleshed and cheerful, but it had sagged under the eyes, under the jaw. There was a good deal of white in his sandy, curly hair.

Tom chose his words carefully. Must be explicit, without divulging too much. "I tell you this in confidence. There has been some suggestion of an association between my daughter and young Upworth and that your son acted as a go-between."

"Is that all?" In his relief Dr Anders took an extravagant gulp.

"It may not sound much — to you. But something depends upon it. If your boy did actually transmit such messages, it mitigates things, a little. If he did not, well, it will influence my action."

"But I told you, on the 'phone; *do nothing*. I can't answer of course for anything Colin did or said. For quite a while now he has been, morally, even legally, quite irresponsible. *This* in confidence, too. My son is at this moment in Fullerton." The name plainly meant nothing to Penfold, and in fact only a few afflicted laymen had ever heard of it. "Fullerton," he explained, "is a place for drug addicts. It claims a fifty per cent success." It also charged just on a hundred pounds a week, because privacy was an expensive commodity and there were façades to keep up; you could be in

91

Fullerton for a nervous breakdown, or for being alcoholic, or even overweight.

"I am sorry," Tom said; and he meant it.

"Well, it happened," Anders said, falling back upon something known as fortitude; symbolised by that Spartan idiot who had allowed the fox — or was it a wolf — to gnaw away his innards while he pretended — and all men were pretenders — that nothing was happening. Fortitude failed sometimes, in the middle of the night and when it did he had nobody to turn to. Felicity was unhappy enough over Colin's breakdown through overwork; if she knew the truth . . .

But in this man he felt that he could at least confide; could perhaps tell the whole story, expose the deadly wound.

He said, "I blame Upworth entirely. He peddles the stuff. Is your girl hooked?"

"Not so far as I know."

"But would you know? That's the point. People are so bloody ignorant."

"I think my wife — she is a nurse. I mean she was."

"Some time ago though. When we were pitying America! If she's all right, not hooked, couldn't you ask *her* for the facts?"

"She's away. A cruise."

"Well, if Colin sat here, we couldn't rely on a word he said. That is a classic early symptom — an ordinarily truthful person becomes a first-rate liar."

Something else to thing about and worry over; Jenny had been more than ordinarily truthful; and that first lie would have been adequate, but for Josh Salter.

"And perhaps to say liar is too sweeping," Anders said, following his own line of thought. "There are hallucinations, too. Colin was once absolutely convinced that he could fly."

"So he might, in what at the moment seemed to him in all good faith, have conveyed messages which in fact had not been given."

"More than likely."

Nevertheless, the note, the snapshot . . . Still, for Tom the vital thing had been the meeting by appointment; the term "ready and willing".

"Is Upworth himself on drugs?"

"Not on your life! Far too smart. Most of his gang are though, that is what gives him his hold . . . And that reminds me. I came thudding over here, partly because I was afraid the boy might have done . . . something I *didn't* know about. But also to warn you. Don't meddle with young Upworth. Whatever he's done. If he raped your girl in broad daylight on the Market Square, do, say nothing. He's dangerous. I know."

Jenny had said the same thing.

"In what way?"

"I only know what happened to me. In confidence, of course." He seemed to settle a little lower in his chair, holding his now empty glass in his hands, turning it round and round.

"Let me freshen that up," Tom said, using the courteous phrase for a refill.

"Well . . . Have you got a biscuit handy? Sorry to be a nuisance, but on an empty stomach . . ."

"Two minutes," Tom said.

He had not lied to Mrs Cooper; he had had a joint in the oven. He hadn't cut into it because he had had no appetite at midday. Left to cool, uncut, all its juices intact, it cut as easily as butter. And going to the kitchen gave him a chance to fiddle with the radio; the laughter had died down. Now some kind of competitive programme, questions, answers, rather dangerously un-noisy for his purpose, but with bursts of applause.

The man was, as old Shaw had always said, a marvel. The exactly balanced tray, the exact manipulation of the swinging door.

"If you'd just pull out the leaf of that table," Tom said. "There we are. It's a bit haphazard, but I'm on my own." On my own, but not alone as the words might imply. The boy was still trying to attract attention.

"I won't bother you," Anders said, "with all the petty details. I'll just tell you . . . He's my only boy, you know; and though I say it, a nice boy. He seemed, at the first, co-operative. I made two mistakes. One, I thought I could treat him myself. Two, I thought I could take action against Upworth. After all, he is a running sore. And I had chapter and verse . . . They're very pitiable, you know — in between bouts. I reckoned I knew about all there was to know — about the organisation. I thought I'd saved my boy and had a duty to others. I had actually made an appointment with Chief Inspector Henderson. On a Wednesday morning; ten o'clock . . . Eight o'clock on the Tuesday, I'd just finished surgery, I had a telephone call. Now there is no doubt about this; it was Upworth. Earlier on when he and Colin had seemed friendly, both keen on motor-bikes, he'd been up to the house a time or two; so I knew his voice. I don't know whether you've ever spoken to him. It is quite distinctive. The voice told me to lay off or take the consequences . . ." He gave Tom a stricken look, fumbled a cigarette from a well-worn packet and lit it clumsily. "Unless I cancelled my appointment with Henderson in the morning I should be charged with misconduct with a woman patient. You know what that means! The BMA has eased off on a lot of things, but it still won't stomach that!" His cigarette was burning lop-sidedly and he tried to level it off on the edge of the ashtray. "I don't like being threatened. What's more, I have an absolutely clear conscience in that regard, so I said they'd need proof of that. Upworth said he had it. The girl kept a diary. And the girl was Mrs John Walter Bridges' granddaughter!"

"Chesford's sacred cow," Tom said.

Mrs John Walter Bridges, old now and retired from public life, was a legendary figure. Her husband had been a prominent man, and had dropped dead while performing some local function. After a brief period of mourning, Mrs J. W. had emerged, black clad and veiled — like Queen Victoria, the perpetual widow — and declared her intention of carrying on her husband's work. She had been one of England's first female mayors. She had still been active, and powerful when Tom came to Chesford and had successfully opposed his first choice of site. Too near the town centre. Her idea of any industrial undertaking concerned itself with

95

tall chimneys, belching black smoke. Tom had disliked her very much.

"Upworth said I had an hour to think it over. Meanwhile look in my letter box."

He threw the unsatisfactory cigarette away and took another. His last.

"There was an envelope, with a photostated copy of a page of a diary. I checked with my receptionist's appointment book. Sure enough, Nancy Bridges had visited me on the evening of Monday, January 8th — she was having a course of injections . . . What is more, on that evening I had been alone — which is rare. I employ two women, a receptionist-secretary, and a retired nurse, kind of general help. Miss Dart had gone to a twenty-first birthday party, Mrs Forbes had turned up, but she was coming down with 'flu, so I sent her home. In the ordinary way Felicity — that's my wife — would have stood in, but she'd gone out before Mrs Forbes felt ill. Now, *who would know all that?*"

He answered his own question.

"Only Colin! You see what I mean? The damed stuff rots them, mind, body, what we used to call the soul. There was I, doing my best for him. My only son — and we'd always been on good terms . . ." He brushed his hand across his tired eyes. "He'd given me his solemn word never to go near Upworth again. And naturally I put no restriction on his movements — for one thing I didn't want his mother to know. So behind my back he went slinking off and helped that vicious young lout to concoct that fieldish trick. My own son!"

Anders paused again, drawing on his cigarette.

"What could I do? The girl is attractive. And that diary was very well faked. Even the fact that no complaint had been made at the time was explained. That day's entry ended, 'I can never tell Gran; it would kill her!' I was trapped, Penfold. I have a wife and three daughters. Get myself unfrocked and what would happen to them? Come to that, what would happen to Colin? I frankly admit that I don't feel towards him now as I once did, and doubt if I ever shall again; but at least I can now just afford to keep him where he has a chance. And I had just an hour in which to decide."

"Terrible."

"Well, I knuckled under. But I still wake in the night and sweat. Looking after one's own, *sauve qui peut*, isn't quite the rock on which civilisation is founded, is it? There're other men's sons and daughters. I simply do not know. Maybe I should have been bolder. But then I think of Mrs Walpole."

"Julia's mother?"

"You knew her?"

"Not Mrs Walpole. Julia. She came here a time or two. She was slightly older than Jenny, but they were friends. Her suicide was a shock."

"Well, yes. Maybe I'm now bending the rules of professional etiquette, Penfold. That was the official verdict — what else could it be; a girl dead in the Park pool amongst the goldfish and the water lilies. Lungs full of water, no sign of foul play. Coroners do whenever possible spare the feelings of relatives. There seemed no need to mention that the girl's thighs were like pincushions. Suicide while her mind was disturbed

— she had just failed some examination. The most merciful verdict."

Tom remembered it, the summer before last; and how he had said to Jenny, in the outwardly flippant way which Jenny understood — and Alice didn't, never had, "Honey, if you ever fail an exam, don't take your own life, take the exam again!"

"Mrs Walpole," Anders said, taking up his tale, "had known, more or less what had been going on. She was a shrewd old Cockney; she started with stalls, selling cheap clobber in markets. Then she set up shop here — better class goods. Rosetta she called herself."

"Yes, I know," Tom said. Almost every article of clothing that Alice had bought, for herself, for Jenny had come from Rosetta's.

"Well, Mrs Walpole went for Upworth, tooth and nail. With police connivance. You see, Penfold, they are handicapped, poor men. They can't just knock on any door and say — Is a cannabis party going on here? And they can't make a search without a warrant. Mrs Walpole knew how to deal with that. She connived with the police, and the police with her. She suspected those Saturday evening parties. So she framed a break-in, a disturbance. Did you ever see her?"

"No."

"Well, she weighed about sixteen stone and had a very loud voice, when she chose to use it. When she made a disturbance, it was a disturbance. And while she was making it the police, with every justification moved in. Raked the whole place over and found nothing incriminating. A lavish party."

He paused again, throwing a backward glance to the unlavish parties by which he and Felicity had managed to keep in the social pond of Hatch End, and another glance to the future in which parties would be decidedly less lavish, and fewer.

"There were," he said, "a few joss sticks — the sort of thing tourists bring back from holiday. Nothing else at all unusual. Mrs Walpole was very angry. She said the police had double-crossed her and tipped Upworth off. She hit two of them with her handbag — a formidable weapon. But of course, she isn't in a psychiatric ward for hitting policemen. Oh no, far more to it."

Tom proffered the cigarette box. "What happened?"

"This you will hardly believe. In fact when Colin told me I thought he was still working the stuff out of his system. He laughed. And you know, he was always such a kind, you might say tender-hearted boy. It's bizarre, Penfold, but it proves my point about Upworth . . . He was annoyed, naturally, by Mrs Walpole's accusations and the police setting foot on his property. She'd ordered a marble angel to stand over Julia's grave — you know what store simple people set by such things. I never saw it, but by all accounts it was quite beautiful and every Sunday morning Mrs Walpole went up to put flowers at its feet. It was defaced."

"Paint?"

"No! Given a great fat pregnant belly . . . I tell you, *he strikes to the heart*, Penfold. This poor old woman — Julia was her last, late-born child, knew about the drugs — not all perhaps, but some, and thought she could effect a cure in a pragmatic way, cut off her

99

allowance. Cut off, the girl drowned herself, and Mrs Walpole was already feeling guilty about *that* — though it is a method that has occasionally worked. With Julia it did not, she was too far gone. So Mrs Walpole did feel guilty, tried to shift the blame — don't we all? And then was faced with this. The final slur on the name of a girl who had at least been decently buried, ostensibly the victim of an iniquitous examination system. In a mother's eyes, tragic but still, on the surface respectable. And Mrs Walpole was nothing if not respectable. She went clean round the bend. Kept demanding an exhumation, an autopsy that would prove that Julia died as virgin as she was born. And you see, Penfold, an autopsy, even after several months, can establish certain things, a bone damage, the presence of arsenic . . . in what remains, but tissues rot. Enough would remain of, shall we say a chemical substance, but Bernard Spilsbury himself could hardly have given Mrs Walpole the one assurance she needed at the moment — that Julia died, poor girl, with her hymen intact. People get obsessions, you know. And that was Mrs Walpole's. She tackled the Home Secretary and finally, the Queen. That was the end. She was put away."

"Horrible," Tom said, "But nothing was known . . . I mean Rosetta's is still there. I pass it every day."

"Business as usual," Anders said. "Mrs Walpole had a son. He took over — with, I may say the maximum of speed and the minimum of fuss. Well . . . I hope I've convinced you that that young man it lethal."

I wonder what you would say if I told you that I have him completely at my mercy, about twenty paces from here.

"You've cleared up something I wanted to know about the messages. I wasn't exactly enamoured with the idea of my girl being involved with a rogue."

Anders eyes narrowed; he was not unaccustomed to being told half-truths.

"Whatever happened; leave him alone. Getting her away was a wise move. Anything more would be folly. He couldn't unfrock *you*, but he'd bring your Works to a standstill, with a flick of a finger."

Precisely what Jenny had said.

"Don't kid yourself it couldn't happen. And don't give me that guff about one big happy family. Bullshit. There hasn't been a happy family on this earth since Eve bore Abel. I know the drill. Yes, sir, no sir, let me kiss your toes, sir, and a gold watch for twenty years' loyal service. But let the temperature drop below the agreed minimum and they'd sing a different tune."

Not possible! All too possible. A mischievous hand on a thermostat . . .

A kind of shudder took Tom. His hands he could steady by gripping the chair arms. But his head jerked, and his jaw.

Poor sod, Anders thought, diagnosing with no brief, and wrongly. Paraplegia. I'd give him three years at the outside.

Sunday, February 5th — Monday, February 6th — Midnight

First of all, absolve Jenny.

That stiff formal little note, the exceptionally good snapshot, had been extorted by some threat.

In some respects Tom had a photographic memory; the note began, "Dear Mr Upworth . . ." Not thus did girls, bent upon dalliance, address boys whose names they know. He should have thought of that!

He strikes to the heart. Anders said; and no doubt about it, with his talk of arranged meetings, of a girl being ready and willing, the wretched boy had struck a blow to Tom's heart, which he had been stupid enough to accept.

He should have had more faith in Jenny. The boy had said something about waiting outside the school; Jenny had said she'd gone out by the side door, into the Park. And I, God forgive me, asked her, *asked her*, if by any chance she was in love with him! No wonder her manner changed. Enough to break her heart!

Absolving Jenny blackened Upworth . . . Add that fluent concoction of lies to what Anders had revealed

102

this evening and it was plain that the boy was very dangerous indeed. Wicked and very clever. The comparatively simple picture of a young lout willing to resort to violence in order to get his own way faded, gave place to something even more sinister; something that should be stopped. But by whom? A liar so skilled — even I half believed him; he almost made me disbelieve Jenny. And a mind subtle enough to plan such an action against Anders, to take such action against Mrs Walpole, would have seen to it that all tracks were well covered.

The police had connived with Mrs Walpole. An action unusual enough to suggest that they cherished some suspicion. But as Anders said they were handicapped. They must have hard evidence. Just as when he had reported a mugging Sergeant Bateson had needed an exact description of the handbag.

Tom was tired, it had been a trying day; but, as had happened before in his experience, exhaustion seemed to give his thoughts a peculiar clarity. He'd often lain awake in the night, gnawing away at some problem, found a solution, and slept. Sometimes the solution needed some slight morning-light adjustments, but he'd had a basis to work upon.

Very slowly as Sunday tipped over into Monday, what had been a personal vendetta inspired partly by anger and partly by the need to know the truth, reformed itself into a kind of one man crusade.

The more he thought about it, the more he thought that it was *just* possible. And he was certainly the only man who could do it.

Before he heaved himself into bed he had made his plan, assembled his apparatus.

Monday, February 6th

The sound of a motor-bike, not a very powerful one. Chug-chug rather than swoosh. But it might be . . . Tom turned the radio on full blast and braced himself.

It was a beautiful morning, the snow down, the sun coming up, and there was Jack, halted by the back door astride a motor-bike. His face matched the promise of the morning.

"I wanted you to be the first, outside the family, to see her, Mr Penfold. Ain't she a beaut? And all due to you. Talk about Musical Chairs! Tell you all about it as we go." Tom said what was required.

"Smashing! You never said a word."

"Well, till Saturday afternoon I wasn't sure. Evie and me . . . Sorry if I'm a bit early. She's no ton-up, but quicker than the old bike."

Through his exhuberance, his joy in his new possession, it had dawned upon him that Mr Penfold didn't look *ready*.

"I've decided not to come in today, Jack. I've got a job that I can perfectly well do here. And there's nothing pending that Higgins can't handle. I'll give him a ring presently."

"You all right?" He didn't look it, Jack thought. Sort of greyish. All on his own here, not eating properly. Jack was a great believer in food, and though Evie was no cook, she was a good provider; the family's consumption of fish-fingers, beef-burgers and such, was prodigious.

Tom assured him that he was in good health, and hoped he would go away. Jack however was not to be done out of the pleasure in telling a story which reflected upon Mr Penfold's generosity, and even more upon Evie's shrewdness. Using her Yellow Stamps as currency she had made some wonderful bargains which had benefited a number of people, each of whom must be mentioned by name. Tom was soon lost in the Laocoon toils. "So you see, everybody's happy," was the joyous conclusion. "Mike's got my old bike and Peter's got young Gedge's. Mrs Stillwater's got her electric iron and Mrs Gedge's old twin-tub, and Mrs Gedge's got a new one. And I got this. She ain't new, of course, but she's been well cared for."

Possibly because his ear was attuned for it, Tom could hear the calling, through the screen of music.

"Wonderful, Jack," he said, heartily, but conclusively. "You tell Evie from me — she should have gone into business."

Jack beamed. "Thass eggsackly what I always said. Now, is there anything I can bring you, Mr Penfold? Go anywhere in the dinner hour, now I'm mobile."

"If I think of anything, Jack, I'll let you know, through Doris, when I ring."

"You do that. Goodbye. And thanks again."

A false start. Engine noise. No noise.

"I forgot to ask. Did that boy bring the car back all right?"

"Perfectly all right."

It was an operation which Jack had faintly distrusted from the start.

"Well . . . good. Goodbye again."

This time he chuff-chuffed away. A happy man.

Who said, "Show me a happy man I'll show you a fool."? Whoever he was, he was wrong, Tom thought, backing into the kitchen. Jack Rogers was a happy man.

Terry, hungry again, and stiff from his second night on the floor, had heard the chug-chug of a motor-bike designed for use rather than display. Peter, he thought, hopefully.

Peter was clever enough to ride a low-powered chug-chug. Peter was the only one of the gang with the sense to say — "If the police cared to, they could count my customers in and out and slow-minded as they are they might wonder at any sudden sign of prosperity. I lack your rich background, dear boy. I also lack Greg's obvious advantages — a well-paid job with lots, and lots of overtime." A sneer there.

Terry knew all about Peter. Son of a poor parson who'd died fairly young. Educated at a school designed for such cases; scholarship to Cambridge, no less. But as he had once explained, it was a glum future — probably as a schoolmaster. BA was valueless now; BSc slightly more marketable but rapidly sinking on an over-glutted market. So he had opted out, and with almost no capital had set up in business; books old and new, with porn under the counter.

And he was following a dream. Italy. Some old, ruined farmhouse in the hills overlooking Florence. To hell with tapped water and plumbing, people had lived happily without them for hundreds of years. Back to nature; the egg straight from the hen; a goat for milk; every man under his own vine . . . So he worked in with the gang and saved, and was mean; he never brought more than a bottle of plonk to the gang gatherings. But he was *clever*.

On this Monday morning Terry, hearing the inferior motor-bike felt a resuscitation of hope. The others might well have taken "out of circulation" as a sign to hold off, do nothing. It was just possible that Peter had seen through it. And come to investigate.

Nothing happened. The motor-bike, its sound muted, chugged away. The frightening silence, and the loneliness, and the hunger took over. He hadn't actually heard the car start, but he imagined that the cripple had gone to work. He made another attempt to free himself and succeeded only in reopening one of the just-healed wounds the dog had inflicted. He had another fit of frenzy — wasted because there was no one to see, or hear and be frightened. It left him limp, exhausted and despairing.

He was relieved, almost pleased when his gaoler appeared. Funny to be glad to see a human face, even this one!

Food too!

Balanced carefully on his knees, Tom had a tray. On it a plateful of cold beef, a tomato. A tomato! A bread roll, butter.

And beside it another slice of the stale bread.

Such indication that he was not to be starved to death after all went to confirm a thought that had come to Terry in the middle of an uncomfortable night.

It had come in a flash. He wasn't being held here for anything he had done, but because of who he was — the son of Upworth, widely believed to have cleared a million on the Stapleford Hall estate alone.

The cripple could be in low water. Terry knew how a business could be to all appearances flourishing while teetering on the verge of bankruptcy. It had happened twice to his father's, but the Old Man, with a good deal of help from Mum, had bluffed his way through and gone on to fortune.

Terry was convinced now that all that yap about Jenny Cooper/Penfold yesterday had been simply a smokescreen. He had been kidnapped, and was now being held to ransom. How much?

Kinky, too. Absolutely no come-back, for the cripple had an alibi, built in. Nobody would believe that a man who couldn't walk, or stand up without aid could kidnap a cat, leave alone a young, strong man. He'd had an accomplice, of course and he'd be miles away now.

Tom looked at Terry with loathing and contempt; Terry looked at Tom with hatred, but with a certain respect, too.

109

"You can have this now," Tom said, handing over the slice of dry bread. "This you can have when I am satisfied that you have answered some questions, *truthfully*. Most of what you told me yesterday was a load of lies."

While Terry devoured the bread Tom busied himself, propping the door open with what looked like a great stone elephant, and then fiddling about as though the exact angle at which the door stood open mattered. The appetising tray he had placed on the little table, just to the side of the door, within sight, out of reach.

"Now," Tom said, swinging his chair into the doorway. "Yesterday you told me that I had the wrong man. But you are Terry Upworth?"

"You know I am." It was not the approach that *his* night thoughts had prepared Terry for. "You know who I am. Old Upworth's son — but you won't get a penny out of *him*. My mother's different. Try her. She could raise twenty-thousand within an hour. And would. To get me out of here."

"Poor woman. I don't doubt it. But it is beside the point. You think you are being held for ransom? No. All I want is the truth."

"But what about? I explained, yesterday, about Jenny."

"As I said — a load of lies. And Jenny can be left out of this entirely. What I'm interested in now is the drug racket you run; the gang you control."

"I don't know what you're talking about."

"Hard luck," Tom said. "Because until you know and tell me, with things I can check . . ." Terry then saw that the cripple had a little black book in one hand, "it's stalemate. Isn't it? Think it over."

With deliberately contrived finality Tom backed his chair away, pushed the stone elephant, let the door slam.

For him it did not seem too long a day. He rang the Works and had a lengthy talk with Higgins, his foreman who, in most other businesses would have exercised far more power than he did in a place where the boss was never absent, never late and never at a loss for an answer. He also talked to Doris who seemed anxious about his well-being. "Honestly, Mr Penfold, when Jack turned up alone, I was worried. I thought you might be ill."

Kind, but maddening. Everybody expected him to be ill.

"And will you be in tomorrow?" Doris asked. "There's that gentleman from the TMC." Doris had her own peculiar hierarchy; at the top the boys — members of the football team; some steep slope below them, men, employed at the works; and at some abysmal low level, the gentlemen who placed orders or solicited them.

"That I can't say for certain, Doris. But the TMC file is ready. If I'm not there, give him that. With my love."

Doris giggled.

"And Doris, I have a message for Jack. Tell him not to come along in the morning unless I send him a message through Mrs Beeson, at the King's Head. If I want him, I'll ask him to come; otherwise he might as well go straight in. Got it?"

The relaying of a message would give Mrs Beeson no trouble at all. Jack was one of her regulars; one of the many Englishmen who, according to the latest theory, drank *warm* beer as a substitute for soup. Thousands of men, married to women like Evie, non-soup makers, men who sought the comfort, the restoration at the end of the day, before going home to the family and the makeshift meal.

After the telephone call, there were the papers, brought by an old man who lived in the Old People's Home at the Ramsfield end of the lane; an indomitable old man who had always earned his keep and still wished to do so. He rode a clumsy old tricycle with a box between its rear wheels. A little late this morning because of the slush.

Even later the postman, with a letter from Alice.

She had written once before, a hasty scribble, written in London, posted in Southampton, saying that she thought darling that you were right. Jenny did seem to be showing a little more interest, and that she hoped Mrs Stamper was looking after him.

This second letter, air-mailed from Las Palmas, might well have been an extract from one of the travel brochures; the weather, the voyage, the flowers were all so wonderful. As he read it Tom thought — Poor Alice, tied to me for ten years, with that one little outing to the Dutch bulb-fields! Jenny, Alice said, was enjoying herself, and sent her love.

Folding the flimsy sheet Tom hoped that Jenny was enjoying herself too much to spare time to write.

After perusing papers and post, Tom set himself to household chores. He felt bitterly remorseful because he had not, long before, bought a second electric chair for use at home. He could have been so much more help to Alice.

He set to work on the living-room grate. Not that he expected to use this room much, but he liked things tidy. He withdrew the panful of ashes and was about to place its contents in the bucket when his hand betrayed him and the grey ash spilled.

Too much stooping, he told himself, stoutly. He'd stooped to put the milk in the lowest shelf of the fridge, stooped over the manipulation of the cloakroom door, stooped over this simple job.

Leaving the spilled ashes where they lay he righted himself and took some deep breaths. And as he did so the telephone rang. By that time he was practically his own man again, remembering other times when stooping had momentarily afflicted him — sometimes even putting on his shoes.

"Hullo," he said. "Penfold here."

"Henderson. Good morning."

"Good morning, Inspector."

They were upon excellent, if not familiar terms. Henderson was a born do-gooder who had often approached Tom to find a job for a man just out of gaol or a man on parole. He was convinced himself, and prepared to argue that such men needed only to be accepted back in society, given a job that restored their self-respect. Tom had occasionally obliged him, drawing

113

a line at baby-bashers but accepting a murderer, a dim-looking little man who had killed his wife and her lover, caught in the act, in a bed that was not yet paid for. He was, Henderson said, quite unlikely to repeat such an offence.

"I rang your office, and was told that you were having a day off. I hope not on account of indisposition." The typical kindly touch.

"Thanks, no. Just a job better done at home."

"Could you spare me ten minutes? A trivial business, but interesting."

"Come right over," Tom said, trying to sound co-operative. The spilling of the ashes had given him a bit of a jolt; now this! Pure coincidence of course, but the fact remained that the last person he wanted inside his house just now was a police inspector whose kindly heart never blinkered his eyes.

He needed a drink, and going over to the table, he poured himself one, downed it quickly, hurried along to the cloakroom and said,

"Hand me your shoes." He should have thought of it sooner.

"What for?"

"If you want to eat today — or tomorrow, do as I say."

Tom hurled the shoes over to join the cistern lid under the window. Then he whizzed into the kitchen and brewed coffee.

"It's about your car, Mr Penfold. Is it in your garage?"

"Why yes. So far as I know."

"When did you see it last?"

"See it? On Saturday afternoon. It'd been playing up a bit, carburettor, I thought. My driver brought me home on Friday afternoon, then drove it back to Corder's. And the young man who runs the place delivered it on Saturday afternoon."

"You saw it?"

"I saw him. I paid him; gave him a tip — very obliging, bringing it back on a Saturday afternoon . . ."

"D'you mind if I take a look?"

"Help yourself. The door isn't locked."

"It should be, you know." It was, in fact from just such remote, seemingly safe places that cars were so easily stolen.

The sun had turned the snow into slush; coming back Inspector Henderson wiped his feet carefully, followed Tom and the coffee pot across the kitchen, through the blare of what was now called music and into the living-room.

"It's there all right." He sounded a trifle disappointed.

"Where did you expect it to be. Stolen? I should have thought my car was about the last one to go missing. Too easily identified. That bar."

"Five minute's work, to an expert, with the proper tools," Henderson said, helping himself liberally to sugar. He then took two good slurps at the sweetened brew.

"Ordinarily," he said, "when somebody free, white . . ." he checked himself, "or black, over twenty-one, goes missing, and there's no suspicion of

115

foul play, or of dodging responsibility for wives and children, we take no action. Why should we? But this morning was slightly different."

"In what way?"

"Well . . . I'll name no names. A young woman, we'll call her Miss X came to see me. She'd been in contact with . . . let's say Miss Y who was much concerned about the disappearance of young Upworth — that's the obliging young man who brought your car back. Miss X apparently had a call on Saturday afternoon; and expected another on Sunday; but it didn't come. So this morning Miss X unburdened herself to Miss Y; and frankly, Miss Y doesn't feel quite the same towards young Upworth as Miss X does. It sounds a bit of a tangle, and I'm sorry to bother you with it. And if anybody asked my opinion I'd say both young ladies would have been far better employed, doing their schoolwork, but that's a thing of the past. What remains is that Miss X was worried about young Upworth and Miss Y thought, hoped, that he'd taken your car. Miss X is obviously worried, possibly infatuated. Miss Y equally obviously, has a grudge, an axe to grind . . . and a bit of legal knowledge."

Kate Dawson?

"Well, he certainly didn't abscond — if he did abscond — with my car. As you have seen for yourself."

"How did he propose to get back to Chesford?"

Just the kind of sly, seemingly innocent question that Alice associated with the police.

"Now, let me see. Yes, he did say something about catching the four o'clock bus. Or failing that, a lift."

Another dead end, Inspector Henderson thought. But he was not only a do-gooder, he was a good man with deep religious convictions which years of dealing with crime and criminals had failed to shake. He knew, because he had experienced it, that occasionally providence made direct intervention with man's affairs. And this might well be one such occasion. He'd come out here on a goose-chase. But look closer. See the uncleared grate, smell the whisky, or the brandy — to a total abstainer the difference was indistinguishable — on this good man's breath.

"Your secretary said you were on your own, Mr Penfold."

"She was correct. My wife and daughter are on holiday. A cruise in the Carribean."

"Is that wise?"

"Holidaying in the Carribean? God knows! They eat and sleep on the ship. When they go ashore they'll be that most precious of commodities — tourists."

"I wasn't thinking of that. I was thinking — here all on your own. Suppose you got ill."

"I'm no more at risk than thousands of other people who live alone. Less, in fact. Fate having seen fit to deprive me of the use of my legs gave me compensation. I enjoy excellent health, Inspector. It is years now since I had so much as a common cold."

Go away, take yourself off before that programme changes.

Henderson said, "If you ever want a bit of help, in the domestic line, there's a good woman, Mrs Stamper;

117

actually in Overby. She is a bit difficult, but if you mentioned my name . . ."

It did not please Tom to crack down on this obviously well-meant offer, but so far as possible he liked to adhere to the truth.

"Mrs Stamper and I are already in touch. I'm to 'phone when I want her."

The Inspector thought that this did not sound like Mrs Stamper — that arbitrary woman; but then, possibly she took Penfold's disability into account and relaxed her rules a little.

"Good," he said. "Oh, and if you'll give me the key, I'll lock that garage door for you."

Two more journeys through the hall and the kitchen! Tom's nerves screamed.

Funny place for a radio, Henderson thought, but from that position and turned on so loudly, it could be heard all over the house, and provided company for the poor devil who was probably feeling lonely.

Kate Dawson had a place in this jigsaw. Being fond of Colin Anders she would naturally feel animosity towards Upworth and wish to see him brought to book on some charge that would stick. Why then had she agreed to be his guest at the House of The Seven Joys? Well perhaps all that and many other things would be revealed, in time. And then, thinking of Kate Dawson, Tom had a flash of almost psychic intuition. Staring at that snapshot he had been emotionally disturbed by the implication of it being in that lout's possession; but his photographic eye had operated unconsciously. Lilies in

118

the foreground; in the background a stone fountain with three long-billed, long-necked birds holding up the bowl into which the water splashed. That was the Dawson's garden. He'd heard descriptions of it. Kate had taken the snapshot; Jenny had written on it for Kate, not for Terry Upworth, and Kate had passed it on. Incidentally, Kate on the evening of that party, had smuggled Jenny away. And kept Jenny's real identity concealed from Upworth. Willing to play along — to an extent. What about that stiff little note? Written because Kate said, "You must," or "Please Jenny." Why?

For Terry it had been a long day, but not unprofitable. Plainly the bleeder knew something about the drugs and the gang, wouldn't be satisfied until he knew a lot more, and had some information to check by.

In order to talk his way out of this, Terry must abdicate from the position he had gained for himself and invent a substitute figure. A mastermind presiding over a network in which Terry Upworth was only a minor, and reluctant part.

Curiously, even in this extremity the thought hurt. But it was obviously useless to say, "I don't know." He must know, and he must tell. Bit by bit — and not without a certain artistry — he invented a scapegoat.

In loneliness, in hunger, in the eerie silence, he worked on the story.

Tom waited until six o'clock.

"Well, have you recovered your memory?"

"I'll tell you all I *know*."

119

"Go ahead. Start with the drug racket."

"I got into it by accident. Doing a good turn. You see, my bike is a good one; even with two up it can make Harwich in under an hour. A friend of mine asked me to run him down to meet the boat from Holland."

"Who is this friend?"

Terry had decided to throw Peter to the wolves. Serve him right for being so supercilious and ungrateful; for what had Peter been before Terry took over? Running his miserable little shop and worried about rent and rates.

"Peter Standish."

Tom pretended to check in his little black book.

"Ah yes, books old new." Tom had never seen Standish; but, wanting a book, long out of print, he had had a telephone conversation with a pleasant-sounding, intelligent man who had said he hadn't a copy but would do his best to obtain one. And had done so.

"And a bit of porn under the counter," Terry said. "I thought Peter was off to collect something that couldn't be printed in England. See?"

"It fits. Go on."

"Well . . . it wasn't books; it was dope."

"How brought in?"

"Dead easy. There's a man in the bulb and seed business. Regular traveller and conspicuous as anybody could be. He wears a black patch over one eye and clothes out of the Ark. And always a baggy umbrella. He's taken for granted, like the ship's funnel."

Old One-Eye was not a figment of a lively, if feverish imagination. He did exist, and he also deserved to be ditched, his charges growing more and more exhorbitant.

"I see; he lands, is summarily searched, if at all. What then?"

"Coming through the barrier he touches his hat. One finger — the Station Buffet; two, the fish and chip shop near the harbour; three, the cocktail bar at the Jolly Mariner. Ringing the changes."

"And then?"

"Well, I only know about Chesford. As I say, I only got into this by sheer accident. But once I was in . . . It was go along or be ruined. Behind all this, Mr Penfold, there's a mastermind at work. Completely ruthless."

With the door propped open, and the radio silenced, the door-bell chimed, loud and clear. Impatient! By the time Tom had backed, fiddled with the door stop, switched on the radio and got himself to the door the chimes had rung three times.

Mrs Cooper!

"Good gracious!" she said. "I was beginning to think your chair must have tipped over, or got stuck in a doorway. Yesterday I was too late — you already had your joint in the oven. I hope I am in time now. I looked out for you this morning — to tell you not to cook; and there was your man on a motor-bike. He told me that you were spending the day at home and I thought . . ." She carried a large wooden box and made for the kitchen setting down the box with a little grunt of relief.

"I don't know how they managed. Two strong footmen, I suppose. It was my grandfather's. He hated a cold meal, even when he was shooting."

"Have you ever seen anything like it? I never did. I think it really should be in a museum."

You too!

She flung open the lid, revealing a number of little containers — silver, lidded, nestling in beds of purple velvet, faded to grey by the suns of bygone years. "Insulation," she said. "The same principle as the hay-box. It's one of Margherita's best dishes. And I couldn't bear to think of you, eating cold meat. So I came early."

"It's extremely kind of you, Mrs Cooper. You really shouldn't have bothered, though. I'll eat it presently. I'm a bit busy at the moment."

Surely she would take that as dismissal.

"Oh, but I intend to eat with you. Going round with Meals on Wheels has taught me something about loneliness. I don't suffer from it myself. I suppose you call me self-sufficient. But many of my poor old dears value a chat more than they do the food . . . Don't break off your work for me. The food will keep hot for an hour. And I shall be quite happy with the paper."

Undoubtedly a woman of goodwill. But Tom disliked being classed with her poor old dears. And he wanted her out of the kitchen. The boy could no longer hammer with his shoe, but even knuckles on a pipe made a noise. And suppose he flushed the lavatory.

"If you are going to give me the pleasure of your company, work must wait," Tom said. "Shall we go through?" He was about to lift the box on to his knees. Get her into the living-room — pity about the hearth! Sit her down with a drink while he fetched cutlery and plates.

"I shouldn't *dream* of it," Mrs Cooper said, pulling the box out of reach. "You mustn't make company of me this evening. I'll just warm some plates. I'm quite domesticated, really."

Tom produced cutlery, making more of a clatter than was strictly necessary.

"While the plates warm, I should appreciate a *tiny* drink," Mrs Cooper said. Strange how women built like battleships and with masterful characters, slipped so easily into girlish, almost coy manners, spattered with diminutives — I'm giving a *little* party: I have a *small* favour to ask.

"How remiss of me. Come through."

Once get her settled in the living-room and he'd whizz back here, load up the whole bang shoot, present her with a *fait accompli*.

"Don't move," Mrs Cooper commanded. "I know where you keep your drinks. What may I bring you?"

He knew what she liked and chose the same. "Whisky and soda, please."

He took advantage of her absence to switch the refrigerator control to its point of maximum performance. It was a fairly old machine and changed gear rather noisily. Having done that he could only hope for the best.

Mrs Cooper, pouring two stiff drinks, observed the spilt ash, the desolate appearance of the living-room. Presently she would have a suggestion to make — when the poor man was mellowed by a good meal.

A good meal it was. Crisp fried chicken; new potatoes from her own greenhouse, the first this year; peas from her own garden, gathered, and into the deep freeze within an hour. Raspberry tart and cream. She chattered away, thank God for that, explaining each item, expounding. Nobody, Tom thought, ever said *I* and *my* so often in a minute. Egotistic, yet not selfish. She asked about Alice, about Jenny. And by some connection which Tom missed, using one of her favourite openings, "I always think . . ." expressed her belief that everybody should have a hobby.

I have one. I keep wicked boys chained up in downstairs cloakrooms!

He said, "I couldn't agree more." And she thought that the time was ripe.

"I've been thinking," she said. "Why don't you come and stay with me, while you're alone. As you know I have masses of help, plenty of room; a whole groundfloor suite, made for my grandmother who had a heart condition in her last years. I could have the whole place aired and ready by tomorrow. Do consider it. Please." Little girl again.

"It's terribly kind of you. I can't possibly accept, though."

"Why not?"

"Need I explain? I can only orbit between this house and my business where everything is geared to my needs. An ordinary bed, an ordinary lavatory, quite useless to me."

"But there is Pedro — and his young brother; I have almost the whole family now — they'd help you."

Again there was that shift inside his head.

"That kind of help, Mrs Cooper, it has been my one aim to avoid."

"Then there is no more to be said."

He had angered her and she was silent as she dropped the containers back into their nests. Then, closing the lid, she cocked her head and said,

"Did I hear somebody call?"

"Yes. Old Salter shouting to his dog."

If he'd thought for an hour he couldn't have given a better answer.

Off she went. "That *terrible* dog! I'm positive that he trains it to poach, and to steal. I no longer rear pheasants, but food is put out from time to time, yet this year, hardly a bird . . . and at least four fowls unaccounted for. Beside it is vicious. I do not believe in allowing a dog one bite and all forgiven and forgotten. I say, once a biter, always a biter. And that cottage is an absolute eyesore. I can never see why an owner-occupier should be given such licence for squalor. If it had been rented property it would have been condemned, years ago."

Her anger with Tom dissipated itself upon Josh Salter and his dog. On the doorstep, under the porchlight her fundamental good nature came uppermost.

"Since you are determined to go it alone, Mr Penfold, how about Mrs Stamper? I can absolutely vouch for her, reliable and honest. Very busy, of course, but I think that if I had a word with her . . . ."

"Very kind," Tom said. "But in fact Mrs Stamper and I already have a workable arrangement."

He had insisted upon carrying out the box; had managed to open the door of the mini and place the box on the passenger seat. He was, obviously far more capable of doing for himself that Mrs Cooper had imagined, and far less grateful than she had every right to expect him to be. He hadn't even eaten very heartily and there was still a considerable amount of food left. Old Mrs Boothby, Mrs Cooper thought; not yet quite nine o'clock; the poor old girl would be just making her cup of Bovril, settling down to watch the news on her old TV set. What a lovely surprise for her.

"You were telling me, when we were disturbed," Tom said. "Once the stuff is in, how is it distributed?"

"Various ways. I only know two. I'm not really in on it, you see. There's the bookshop and Stan's place."

He felt that it was safe to give these two away. Peter's passport was in order and at the first hint of trouble he'd get out, not bothering to ask who had betrayed him. Stan would bluff it out. Stan was a veteran; he'd say that the stuff had been planted on him — that is if any were found; he'd say the police themselves had planted it; that the police had a down on him simply because he had a bit of a record. He'd raise a fine stink! And even if he did discover that Terry was a traitor, he'd bear no grudge; all in a day's work, he'd say. He couldn't afford to fall out with the gang whose

126

strong-arm methods offered protection against rough customers.

Also there was the fact that if the cripple made use of this information — extracted under torture! — there'd only be *his* word for it. Of course the police would prefer to believe a toffee-nosed bastard. Even so they'd be bound to concentrate on the mastermind of Terry's invention.

The great thing — indeed the only thing that mattered — was to talk his way out of here.

"And from those centres of distribution how does it reach those who use it?"

"That was well thought out," Terry said, settling in to praise himself. "Peter makes up a book title and it's circulated about. You go in there and ask for that book; he says it isn't in stock but he'll try to get it for you, and you say you'll have a paperback to go on with. You choose one and Peter says he'll put it in a bag for you, and the stuff's already in the bag. Simple. It's been done with a copper in the shop, getting a paperback for himself." And who thought up this simple method? Not Peter Standish, BA Cantab, but Terry Upworth who had never taken, leave alone passed, an examination in his life.

"Then how is he paid?"

"It depends. If the shop's empty, there and then. Anybody Peter knows and'll be seeing later, settles up when they meet. Other times he'll say, 'That'll be 30p; together with what you owe on account it makes . . .' Well, whatever the going charge is. And whatever it is, they pay. No pay, no further dealings."

"That is what happened to Julia Walpole?"

Terry's eyes widened a little. How the hell did the bastard know about *her*, dead and buried eighteen months ago and her old woman in the funny house.

"Most likely. You see, the man behind all this, he says he isn't running a charitable institution. He's a very tough fellow indeed."

Tom's turn to be surprised, introduced thus abruptly to a new character.

"Who is he?"

"Honestly, I don't know, Mr Penfold and I can't tell you what I don't know, can I now? I only saw him once. And that was when he made clear to me that running Peter down to Harwich — I explained how that happened — I'd committed myself and unless I went on meeting Old One-Eye and bringing the stuff in, he'd ruin me. What could I do?"

"And where did you see him? In what circumstances did he make this threat?"

"At his place. In the country somewhere."

"Where?"

"I don't know. Peter just said that he and me were asked to a party and could we go on my bike. So we went and Peter said, go left, go right and I took his directions: It was a lonely place. Nice when you got there. Beautiful old country house. I saw that much."

"And the man?"

"Oh very handsome. But sinister. Foreign, though he spoke good English. And there was a party and I enjoyed it, till he took me aside and explained . . ."

"Tell me about it. About him."

All the elements of all the XX books, all the fantasy poured out. The human imagination — and Terry had his full share — is incapable of pure invention; it can lean backwards and make horror out of the peaceful, herbivorous dinosaur, or lean forward and envisage space travel, but nothing *new*. Try to describe a new animal and you say it had a horse's head, a lion's paws and a camel's hump. The first attempts to fly were made by a man with imitation bird wings. Icarus, whose wax-held wings melted in the sun.

Tom thought these things as he listened, slightly, but not entirely sceptical; for it was a fact that the notorious Kray brothers had occupied, and operated from, much such a house as Upworth described; remote, moated, with panelled walls and chandeliers.

"But you don't know his name?" he asked at last.

"He has a dozen, most likely . . . Mr Penfold, can I have something to eat now? I've told you what I know. And I am starving."

Tom lifted down the tray but as he held it out his hand failed again; the thing tilted and slid its contents on to the floor. The boy grovelled like a dog, snatching up the food from the mess of broken crockery, the spilled salt, the tomato which had burst as it hit the floor. Tom watched and was slightly appalled by the satisfaction he felt. — Yes, inside ourselves we all cherish a little sadist; and I enjoy seeing somebody who attacked Jenny and lied about her thus reduced.

And then, for some reason, inscrutable even to himself, he felt ashamed; and went to the cupboard under the stairs and dragged out the sleeping bag which

Jenny had taken with her when she went on a camping holiday with the Dawson's, in the Dordogne region of France. It was one of the best sleeping bags money could buy; fleece-lined. Tom couldn't go with Jenny, couldn't share the holiday; the least he could do was to provide. Pulling it out of the orderly cupboard which Alice had always said must *not* become a junk hole, Tom felt some compunction; it was blue, it was Jenny's. But he was reasonably certain now that if the wretched boy had not fully possessed her body, he had almost done so — so why not her sleeping bag.

He flung it down without speaking.

Tuesday, February 7th

Tom had had a bad night. Mind in a rut, going over and over the story he had been told. His usually effective sleeping pills brought only brief snatches of sleep from which he woke, every time to the same thoughts, the same examination, the same question. How much, if any of it was true? He tried to read; tried to think of other things, but between him and the page, between him and even business thoughts, the story and the mental images it evoked would obtrude.

Well, up to a point the thing could be checked.

Impatience drove him to telephone Inspector Henderson at his home. For that and the earliness of the call, he apologised.

"Quite all right. I've just finished breakfast. What is it?"

"I wondered if you'd know of a place, roughly within this area, where a man of foreign origin lives in great splendour."

"Grinley Park." The answer came promptly. Henderson knew his beat. "Ali Mahomet Khan. Parkistani from Uganda."

"At Grinley Park?" Tom's ideas of refugees from Uganda were limited to those poor people who had been kicked out — after they'd been stripped of possessions.

"Shrewd man," Henderson explained. "He sniffed the wind of change before even Macmillan did. Got out when the going was good. Very rich from all one hears. Grinley was practically derelict, now it sounds like the Taj Mahal."

It fitted. Foreign, wealthy. And didn't all drugs originate in the East?

"What's he like?"

"Like? Very decent little bloke."

"Little?" Terry's mastermind operated in a tall handsome body.

"Physically, I mean. Poor in early life; too much rice. I'd say rickets; knobbly head. Curvature of the spine."

"Then I don't think he's my man," Tom said. "Look here, Inspector, I'm sorry to sound so vague, but I can't very well be specific without making a breach of confidence."

He could have done. One of his night-thoughts had toyed with the idea of saying that this mysterious foreigner had come to his office, announcing himself, in broken English, by a name that neither Doris nor he had fully caught. But he had discarded that idea because it involved lying and he still wished to avoid, as far as possible, the unnecessary lie.

"I understand," Henderson said. In his day he had received many half-confidences, some very helpful. But not from people like Tom Penfold. "Tell me what you can."

"Well; the house is moated; very remote. Wooded country. Tall iron gates, And as I say, very splendid. Chandeliers, the lot."

Knowing so much about the place why didn't Penfold know where it was, or who occupied it? Henderson's practical mind shelved that thought for a while and he said,

"Moated? There aren't so many of them, now. There was Farley Grange — but they filled it in and planted asparagus. Frog's Hall at Flaxham, but you couldn't call Brigadier Jameson foreign. Cockshurst Old Hall, and you couldn't call that grand. All I can think of at the moment. Look, Penfold, you've done me many a favour in the past, and I'll help if I can. Could you just tell me the *connection*."

"A demand for more credit than I feel disposed to give — off-hand."

"Oh!" Henderson said.

It was a tip-off. Some foreign agent, placing an order with Component Parts. Penfold suspicious. Suspicious in his turn, he asked,

"Are you all right?"

Tom thought sourly — He thinks I'm drunk. Abstainers did so tend to think that anything slightly out of the ordinary implied drunkenness.

"Absolutely."

"Alone?" Nobody would have thought it, twenty, even ten years ago, but things moved so fast now. Outrages nobody ever dreamed of — hijacking, kidnapping, telephone-bugging. Penfold's tight-mouthed query might be an underhand warning.

"Yes."

"I'll make a few inquiries and ring you back from the office. Where'll you be in say an hour's time?"

"Here. Thanks."

"Saunders, old buildings are your hobby, aren't they? You wrote that article for the Free Press. Can you tell me, off-hand, any moated house, in this area, apart from . . ." Henderson repeated the names.

"Yes, sir. Nag's Cross."

"Where's that?"

"Two miles off C32, sir. East. In the middle of the forestry land."

Wooded. Remote.

"Occupied?"

"It was, sir, when I took photographs — for my article. Two foresters. But their wives weren't happy. Too lonely. They may have been rehoused. I wrote that article three years ago, sir."

"Could it be called a splendid place?"

If you'd really read the article, looked at the photographs, you'd know that even in decay it had a grandeur seldom seen.

"In the right hands, sir."

"Thanks, Saunders. Hop out there and see if it's in the right hands. Report straight back to me."

On a cold, but bright morning, with a promise of spring in the light if not in the air, what more desirable assignment could a young man want? But sad, in the end. The forester's wives had evidently got their way. The grand old Tudor house, far from being in the right

134

hands, was in no hands at all. Dead and deserted, and the nettles and brambles shoulder high.

Disappointing. Because, consulting a large scale map, Henderson had seen that the Forestry Commission's land verged on the Brakeland, flat, rabbit-nibbled, lonely. You couldn't land a Jumbo Jet there, but you could a less demanding aircraft . . .

Well, that had been a hunch, a flight of fancy; Component Parts and God knew what else being flown out by some foreign agent who had put up a front of grandeur.

There were other resources. Rates! Every inch of property in England was rated. Having made his flight of fancy, Inspector Henderson came back to solid ground and made contact with the rating authorities in Chesford and with all those who might be regarded, however loosely, as within his area. The bag was not large; three Chinese paid rates on their restaurants; the County Council had made two of its houses available to Ugandan refugees; an Italian had taken over a mushroom farm at Flaxham — and was building a bungalow.

Tom telephoned the Works and spoke to Higgins who was almost sycophantic, who actually said, "We miss you." All well there. He then finished cleaning the grate and Hoovered the rug. Again he was amazed at the extra handiness conferred by the electric chair. He must order another one for home use.

He was watering the plants when the Rolls-Royce whispered to a standstill. Beautiful shape, horrible colour, a kind of dead violet. A chauffeur in a matching uniform, stepped out and rang the bell. Tom turned on the radio and went to the door. Then, and only then, did the man open the rear door. A woman, somewhat impeded by mink, by a huge crocodile handbag, by what looked like twenty gold bracelets, and by her own bulk, heaved herself out and stood on fat legs which sloped steeply down to tiny feet shod in crocodile. Her face was made up to the fondant pink-and-white of an earlier time, her mouth a rose-red Cupid's bow.

Her manner was surprisingly brisk and businesslike.

"Mr Penfold? I'm Mrs Upworth. Sorry to be so early. I did ring; first your office, then here. Twice. Number engaged both times."

He ushered her into the living-room, glad that he'd cleaned it. Even so it made a strange background for so much opulence and the aroma of Chanel No. 5.

She sat down on the settee and came straight to the point.

"Mr Penfold, do you know anything about my boy — Terry?"

"I? What could I know, Mrs Upworth?"

"Well; he was last heard of here; Saturday afternoon. I'd better explain. It's no secret, everybody in Chesford know that Terry and his Dad fell out. But he's still my boy and I ring his garridge every Sunday morning. Wet or fine, his Dad's at the Golf Club then. *This* Sunday there wasn't no answer; nor yestiddy, nor this morning — I tried while his Dad was shaving. The point *is*, Terry never said nothing to me about being away. He know I'm a worrier and when he's going to be away, he'll tell me. So I rung one of his friends — so-called, and she said the last anybody knew was he brought your car back, Saturday afternoon. So I did wonder did he happen to say anything."

"He proposed to catch the four o'clock bus from Overby. Or failing that, thumb a lift."

"He didn't say nothing like, 'Me for the lights of London!' Or 'Look up, Leicester, here I come.'"

"No. Nothing like that."

"Then you can't help?"

"I'm afraid not. I'm sorry."

"Well . . ." she said, "that's that then." She took out a fine, much laced, heavily-scented handkerchief and twisted it in her plump hands; all the bracelets jingled.

They sat silent for a moment — reassessing one another.

Daphne Upworth had always been given to understand that Tom Penfold was a surly, unsociable man able to ignore his affliction where business was concerned, unwilling to make an effort outside it. Wouldn't be a Mason, or a Rotarian or a non-playing member of the Golf Club.

Tom had — God forgive him, had thought Daphne Upworth as something of a joke. Something she'd once said in a speech when she was Mayoress, had gone the rounds. Mrs Cooper had told Alice. The speech had concerned industrial expansion in Chesford and the Mayoress had said, "We want to be in the front rank, not in the van."

Now they saw one another differently. She saw him as a nice, kind, understanding gentleman, very different from Joe! She realised that she had always had a sneaking weakness for the well-spoken, the courteous. She'd had her idols — she'd been an usherette in a cinema when she'd caught Joe Upworth's eye. And thought herself lucky; been much envied . . .

Tom saw her as pitiable, despite all the grandeur.

"I don't think you should worry over-much, Mrs Upworth. I don't know your son well — I've only just begun to use his garage — but I'd say he was well able to look after himself."

"Good, big, strong boy. Well, I saw to that. Not much sense, though. And very easily led. Even as a child. Every bit of mischief he got up to he was led into, if you see what I mean. And now he's off I don't know where, I don't know who with. He's my one and only . . ." She managed a small, deprecating smile.

"The young are very careless, Mrs Upworth. My one and only has been away for more than a week — and not so much as a picture postcard . . . May I give you a drink?"

On her other plump wrist she wore a watch-bracelet, the band thicker, the face smaller than any he had ever seen. She consulted it.

"It *is* a bit early, but tell you the truth, I could do with a gin."

"With vermouth? Tonic? Choice a bit limited, I'm afraid."

"Straight, please. You see I've been on the agitate since Sunday and it's got me down a bit. Nobody to talk to, really, his Dad not feeling as I do. Thanks. Happy Days . . ."

138

The telephone yelled.

The call from Henderson.

Hell! Tom thought. He said, "Excuse me."

Inspector Henderson.

"So far, absolutely no trace. I've tried everything. Alien registration, application for naturalisation, jump in rateable value when an old place is improved. Not a clue. Could it have been a hoax?"

"Very likely."

Cloak and dagger stuff was not in Henderson's line — but neither was this tight-lipped stuff in Tom Penfold's line. Concise, yes, but never cagey.

"But what would be the point?"

"To waste my time — and yours. About that I am truly sorry."

"Look Penfold, I've no wish to be nosey, but is this, however remotely, something *I* ought to dig into?"

"Good God, no. Further waste of time."

Something wrong about this conversation. Stilted. And Penfold hadn't once said either "Inspector" or "Henderson." Almost as though . . .

"Penfold, are you alone?"

"As a matter of fact, no. I'd just poured a lady a drink and was about to pour myself one. Thanks a lot for trying. Goodbye."

"Sorry about that." Tom turned back. "Let me just freshen that up."

She was an experienced drinker, tipping down the undiluted gin as though it were water, but under the

139

pink-and-white, high on the cheekbones a darker colour was creeping.

"What worries me," she said, "is the lot Terry runs around with these days. There his Dad was right and there's no gainsaying. They sponge on him and they do wild things and nine times out of ten Terry get the blame. You know how it is — give a dog a bad name. Like setting fire to old Porter's chicken-house."

"I don't think I heard about that."

"Well . . . Porter's is the last place out on the Stoke Martin Road. Dead Straight and not much traffic, so the boys used it as a sort of race track. For the bikes. Hens, in case you don't know, go to bed early, so do people who keep them, like old Porter and his wife. So he didn't like the bikes, and complained. Maybe there ain't a law against keeping people awake, but there's speed limits. Terry got hisself fined — but so did three more, Colin Anders — the only decent other one — amongst them. Some bit later Porter's place went up in smoke. And everybody said — Terry Upworth getting his own back. Not, mark you, Colin Anders, or that Greg Hawes, or Jerry Wall — they'd all been fined just the same."

"One wonders why not."

She was not accustomed to the company of people of who said "one" when they meant "I" or "you" and it took her a second to work it out.

"Dead easy. Matter of class."

"Class, Mrs Upworth?"

"Colin Anders — doctor's son; and you never know when you might want a doctor. Greg Hawes and Jerry

Wall, great stupid louts, working class, too stupid to strike a match. So what are you left with? Terry Upworth — bad boy, couldn't even get along with his father. See what I mean. 'S' matter of fact it couldn't have been Terry. That I know for a fack. He was up in Leicester, chasing some bitch — but that time he let me know. Now he didn't and so I worry. And come bothering you . . ." She gave that small, self-deprecating smile again. Tom felt the compunction that came so easily to him.

"I'm sure you'll hear soon, Mrs Upworth."

"Well," she said, heaving herself up, "I surely hope so. Apart from all else, it don't do a garridge no good, closed Monday and Tuesday — best time for lorries. Thanks for the drink, Mr Penfold. And for listening."

Outside she reverted to her crisp manner.

"Dixon, if you'd turned round while you waited, you'd have saved time."

Indoors the telephone shrilled again.

It was Higgins who had so often resented not being given more responsibility and now faced with it didn't care for it much. Tom could solve his problem without reference to anything but his memory.

"Will you hang on, sir. Doris wants a word."

Doris's problems were more complicated, needed reference to papers and something of the personal touch.

"I'll see to it all, Doris. Not to worry. Yes, yes, I'm quite all right. Nothing I need, thanks. See you soon."

141

He went along to his own room where on the desk there were the papers he needed, and also the business telephone numbers.

He dialled carefully; even with his memory and aptitude for figures, he found the new system a bother. He had a moment's nostalgia for the days when a place name and a mere four or five digits sufficed. The place names had also guarded against confusion between identical numbers in differing areas.

Despite his care he was met with the almost inevitable, "Hullo, Phyl," a female voice ready for a cosy chat. Mechanisation, supposed to be man's servitor, had become master.

The first call led to another, and that to a second, third and fourth; two of them delayed by the "number engaged" signal. But it was done at last, and as he put the telephone down and was about to visit the boy, he heard sounds and a voice calling, "Mr Penfold!"

The radio was silent; he'd switched it off when he closed the door on Mrs Upworth!

Never had the chair moved to fast! He whizzed it along, turned knobs without selectiveness, thanked God for Lunchtime Music, and pushed into the kitchen, whence the voice had come.

Jack and Doris; their noses red, their eyes watery from travelling through the cold at the best speed of which the old machine was capable.

Doris clutched to her bosom a bulky parcel wrapped in insulating material.

"It's fish-and-chips, Mr Penfold," Doris explained. "I happened to go into the canteen, and it was plaice. It

142

looked so nice and I thought of you, all on your own. So I asked Jack . . . I nearly laughed when you said you'd see me soon!"

Her manner was jaunty. Jack was aware of the fact that he'd been told not to come until he was sent for and was slightly sheepish.

"We hoped you wouldn't mind."

"Mind? Why should I mind? What a kind thought!" The heartiness sounded forced and hollow. "I settled that business, Doris. I'll ring you this afternoon."

"You can tell me while we eat, Mr Penfold," Doris said, absent-mindedly. Her attention was elsewhere. With a woman's inbuilt capacity to be at home in *any* kitchen, she was assembling plates and cutlery.

While we eat. Tom did his best to conceal his dismay.

Nothing unusual about that. In the canteen, picking his table at random, he'd eaten with them both, many times. And Doris's arrangement was logical; by the time they were back at Chesford their meal would be past its prime.

Tom remembered that many man liked vinegar on the dish known as fish-and. He found a bottle and put it on the table. Doris opened the parcel, steam and an appetising odour emerged. She allocated the generous portions. Last night he had not done full justice to Mrs Cooper's meal; this morning he felt bound to say, "Doris, please; too much! You split that third piece between you and Jack. You've been in the air, working up an appetite. Give Jack a few more chips. Well, what's the latest gossip. How did Chesford get on on Saturday?" Always a safe subject.

143

"We lost." She told why. Foul play on the other side. The dirtiest play she'd seen in all her days, and a referee no more good than a sack of potatoes — unless he'd been got at, which was more than likely. A team that would do such things on the open field wouldn't stop at anything.

Doris had mastered the art of eating and talking at the same time. She moved things on the table to illustrate her point; she gave exact imitations of insulting or defiant voices; what they had said, what we had said, what she had said herself — including the cogent question, "Man, what's that whistle for?" It was satisfactorily noisy.

Jack also had news. Evie had again given proof of her cleverness.

"There ain't much get past Evie, Mr Penfold. Mrs Cook dropped in for a cuppa, yesterday morning; but mainly to tell Evie that her Freddy'd just bought hisself a car, and Evie said, sharp as sharp, 'Then he won't want his skid-lid no more, will he? I'll give you twenty pee for it.' So now I am set up. It's a bit red for my liking but that can't be helped."

In Jack's world fish-and should either be accompanied, or quickly followed by, a cup of good strong tea. He offered to make it. "No, Doris, you sit. Ladies' privilege."

Over the brew more news emerged,

"By the way, Corder's is shut again. Closed yesterday, and today." So no more of that nonsense. Blake's in future. And more Yellow Stamps.

"And all sorts of tales going round," Doris said.

Too late, Jack perceived his errors.

144

"There's always tales," he said.

But Mr Penfold seemed interested.

"Such as?"

"There's a car missing. Mr Burwash's, out at Hatch
End. They're saying Terry Upworth took it. And if he
did it wouldn't be the first time, would it?"

"You mean he had taken Mr Burwash's car before?"

"No. He took his own father's. Years ago. He'd
failed his driving test that day and he was savage —
I know because Charlie Webb — he was one of the
testers then, and he played for Chesford, about the
best goalkeeper we ever had. He said nobody ever
took a first failure so hard. Terrible language, he
said. So that night, I suppose to show that he could
drive, Terry Upworth took his father's car. And
wrapped it round a tree out at Flaxham. A Jaguar it
was too, and brand new."

Doris suffered none of the inhibitions imposed upon
Jack by Evie's dislike of gossip about the family to
which she was, however tenuously, related.

"Old Upworth made nothing of it. That time he was
as dotty about Terry as his mother was. It wasn't till
that phoney break in . . . Whatever may be said about
Old Upworth, he is devoted to his wife."

As a man should be! Doris, never fortunate enough
to command a man's devotion, none the less rated it
highly; the ultimate goal of a woman's life. Somewhere,
some celestial referee had given the decision against
her, from the very start, no looks, no figure. But like a
good player, she'd borne up, played on. "It wasn't till

145

Terry mugged his mother, of all people, that his father had done with him."

Jack said, "Come on, Doris. Time we got back." And then, because Mr Penfold appeared to be attending to Doris's gossip, he said, "Mr Penfold, you got a knocking pipe. It started up when I filled the kettle."

"I know. Some fault in the plumbing. It knocks. Now and again it makes peculiar sounds — like somebody calling. Once I thought it was a cat or something in a trap."

"All traps," Doris said, "should be forbidden by law. A few of us are getting up a petition about it. All the boys will sign, that I do know."

"I don't know about pipes," Jack said. "But Wilson's a good plumber. Would you like me to run him out, Mr Penfold?"

"No. I can deal with it, Jack. Once I get around to it. It's gone cockeyed. Sometimes it will even flush itself."

It was doing so now.

Doris was not interested in plumbing. She was gathering the meal's debris and shooting it into the wrapping of paper and stuff. *Take your litter home.* Over the washing-up, Tom forestalled her.

"Leave it Doris. Somebody takes care of all that."

"Want me tomorrow, Mr Penfold," Jack asked.

"If I do, I'll let you know. It all depends upon whether I get this bit of work done or not. If you don't hear from me, no."

Doris, tying her head-scarf, said, "Is it an invention, Mr Penfold?"

"Well," Tom said, "I suppose it is, in a way."

146

★　★　★

Despite the meal, the relatively comfortable bed, the boy looked poorly.

Tom had a thought about survival. Divide people into white, black, brown, male, female, young, old, clever, stupid, good, bad, chop, chop, chop and only the age-old cleavage never varied. There were survivors, and non-survivors.

He'd seen it happen in Korea where he'd done his conscript National Service. Eight men, completely cut off for five days; no food, no contact, and very little water. Circumstances had been the same for all; even the last cigarette shared, passed around. When rescue came three were dead; they'd given up, curled into a foetal position and died. Five for no obvious reason, not the biggest, not the youngest, alive and if not well, prepared to be — tomorrow.

That was long ago. But Tom had seen the same thing twice since; once in Africa, once in Brazil.

The boy was obviously a non-survivor. And Tom's carefully laid plans did not include the disposal of a corpse.

Terry's last hope of rescue, even of police intervention had died as time passed, and as the chug-chug of the lower-powered bike led to nothing. He had, for a moment thought that it could be Peter, after all. He'd hammered on the pipes with his fists, and shouted, flushed the loo. All to no end. He'd concocted, yesterday, yes, yesterday, a good story which the cripple had seemed to accept. But plainly hadn't — otherwise he would either have turned him loose or fetched the police. But there was nothing. Nothing. Two o'clock. Another two hours and he'd have been in this place for three whole days. Nancy hadn't bothered to give the boys the clue. Sheer spite because he'd never fooled about with her — not even at the most promiscuous party. Or she had told them, and they'd taken no notice. All jealous of him, really, in their hearts, wanting to run the show themselves. Lot of big-heads; couldn't run a coffee stall! They'd learn!

But where shall I be then?

He had another fit of frenzy and after that, flaccid and pallid, and dull-eyed, faced Tom.

No real stamina, Tom thought; and leaving the door propped wide, swung himself into the kitchen, made strong coffee and, remembering his mother's cure for anything short of a broken bone, spread honey liberally on buttered bread.

"Get that down," he said ungraciously.

As Terry ate and drank Tom watched and meditated. "My one and only." But if the boy had cared two pins about his mother he'd have remembered all those Sunday mornings and asked could a message be got to her. Tom himself had been so aware of her anxiety that waiting for a call to get through he'd thought that if only he had some gift of mimicry he'd have rung the poor woman, aped Terry's voice and reassured her.

The cure worked. Something in Terry revived.

"I was beginning to think you meant to sarve me to death."

"You'd be no use to me, dead. Dead men don't talk. And I want you to talk."

"But I did. Yesterday. You said I could go if I told you what I knew. And I did tell you."

"You told me a lot of lies. Not a bad story, I admit. In fact I think you've missed your proper vocation. You could out-Bond James Bond with one hand tied behind your back."

Susceptible to flattery, even now. The shallow brown eyes brightened.

"But not original enough, Upworth. Moated houses in dense woods! Chandeliers! handsome foreigners! All as dead as the Dodo! And all open to proof. There's no such man, there's no such place. Try again and let's have the truth this time. I've wasted enough time. Your business isn't flourishing either. Though perhaps that doesn't matter to you — you have other sources of revenue, I imagine . . . I am about to suggest, to you that the mastermind is yours; that the whole organisation is yours."

"If I said so, *if* . . . What then?"

"Once my curiosity is satisfied you will be free to go."

"You mean that?"

"I usually mean what I say."

"But how? Wouldn't you be afraid of what I might do?"

"Attack me? Hardly. For one thing you're far too clever to do that. For another, I don't set much value on my physical safety. Would you? In my place?"

"I could go to the police. What you've done to me since Saturday is dead against the law."

149

"You *would* look silly! Me, in a wheel-chair; with at least fourteen reputable people ready to swear that for ten years I haven't taken a step, or stood up without support. You'd be a laughing stock! Come on now, settle for the truth, and off you go."

"You mean that?"

"Didn't I say so from the first? The blunder over my daughter's name was feasible. I accept that and, as I said, we'll leave her out of this entirely. And I don't want any more rubbish about mysterious foreigners. Just for once, try to tell the truth. We've dealt with the bookshop. And with Harwich. Now I want to know the rest. Stan's for example, where the stuff is hidden, how dispersed? Why everybody is so frightened of you; how you managed to get away with firing Porter's chicken-house, for instance, I want it all, on the nail."

"But what for?"

"Because I say so. I'm asking the questions. And you answer them or . . . Or tomorrow I shall leave. Close the house down and leave you here to starve and rot. It's not the course I should choose, but if you won't tell a story that will stand up, I have no alternative. Go ahead — and remember, I can check."

Terry thought — He'd do it, too, the inhuman bastard! Ruthless himself, he recognised that quality in others.

And how the Hell could the cripple have made so certain, in so short a time, that the man and the place, so carefully described, did not exist?

Equally bewildering, how had he made the connection with old Porter's place, when even the police had failed to do it.

Sitting here, knee to knee with the boy, Tom had made some observations. Fluency, a willingness to talk was in inverse proportion to the truthfulness. The lies about Jenny's encouragement of him had flowed freely, so had the story of the mysterious foreigner; the account of the bookshop — probably true — had had more reluctance about it. The cover for the illicit trade was well devised; and the boy was abnormally vain. Could it be that he hated — at least subconsciously — not to claim the credit for it?

Somewhat in the manner of a barrister leading an unwilling witness, Tom said,

"I'm going to put it to you again, Upworth, that in all these doings there was no other mastermind at work except your own." Unbelievably, this statement brought about that same brightening of the eyes as the remark about James Bond had done. The boy was a megalomaniac!

Laying it on thickly, Tom said, "That bookshop drill is well-devised. How does the café work?"

"Well, much the same. There's a lot of people who'd look a bit odd, and feel a bit silly in a bookshop. They go to Stan's."

"How did you enlist him?"

"Easy. His is a poorish sort of place and he had some rough customers. He couldn't deal with them himself — getting old, and he wouldn't go to the police because he's got a bit of a record. So we took over . . ."

If you must tell the truth or die you might as well get the credit. Terry's eyes gleamed again.

151

"They soon learned. Some of my boys are pretty hefty. Start a smash-up at Stan's and you're likely to end smashing up yourself."

"And in return he is a distributor. How?"

"Well . . . He knows his regulars, of course. They get it in their cigarettes, or instead of salt in the twists of paper. He always serves salt like that — salt-cellars being so liable to be used as ash-trays, and shakers always clogged. Anybody new, unknown to Stan has a password, like with the books. They say "Doc". Stan, Stanley, Livingstone. Doctor Livingstone, I presume." Perversely, Terry was proud of that touch.

"Very clever," Tom said, stoking the megalomaniac fire.

"And harmless. After all we're only giving people what they ask for. In a couple of years it'll be legal. Like abortion or the arse-mongers."

"I have a lot to learn," Tom said. He felt, dismally, that he had come a long way from his starting point which was to teach a young lout a lesson and find out the truth about Jenny. And every step had plunged him deeper into a morass of filth. Of intelligence misdirected.

Automatically he sought comfort. His pipe. With the door to the hall open and the ventilator going a pipe would do no harm.

Before filling it he gave it a little scrape with a tool, designed for the purpose, which was attached to his key ring. A present from Jenny.

Terry watched, and presently smelt. Early on in his incarceration he had craved for a cigarette, but the craving had died down and he thought he had kicked that addiction, his one weakness. The use of drugs he had sedulously avoided, and about alcohol he had always been cautious, having seen its effects first on his father and then on his mother. It made them silly and sometimes quarrelsome. He could take a beer with the boys, and he liked a glass of decent wine with a decent meal — and if the wine happened to be from a bottle snitched by Nancy from her grandmother's cellar, the enjoyment was enhanced; tasting of power. Power. The one thing that mattered.

Unwittingly Tom had also struck at the heart.

Reduced to impotence, to pleading, the boy said, "Could I have a cigarette?"

"I don't see why not. This is going to be a long session."

From his other pocket Tom produced a rather crumpled packet, and a lighter.

And then, relentless as the Hound of Heaven, in an atmosphere almost cosy, Tom pursued his quarry.

"Where is the stuff kept?"

Slight hesitation; truth likely.

"At Stan's in a swill tub with a double bottom. The worst stinker of the lot. Even the man who buys swill for his pigs complains."

"Most apt! Yes, that fits. And at your place?"

"I don't keep it. I'm not a fool. I don't have it used on my premises, neither." He looked smug.

Tom glanced at his book.

"The police gave your place a good going over. Clean as a whistle. But you fetch it, assign it here and there . . ."

Staring at the blank page Tom was visited by inspiration. Not in the house — and while they had their noses in the police would have inspected the workshop, too. Workshop!

"I'll answer that for you," he said, thinking the risk worth taking. "At the bottom of the inspection pit. Under an oily rag."

A glance at Terry's face informed him that he was correct.

Even within the gang, Terry had been cagey, and only two people knew that. Colin Anders because he was so hooked that it had seemed safe to trust him — an assumption that had proved false, and yet, finally, true: and Greg. Anders was safely locked up. Greg then. Judas! Kerist, if ever I get out of here! And then, for perhaps the first time in his life, Terry Upworth felt a flash of sympathy. It could be that somebody was wrenching information out of Greg as this bastard was wrenching it out of him. Two of them at it, one working on Greg, one on him, and comparing. Over the telephone.

"Who's doing the brain-washing job on Greg?"

"I ask the questions here," Tom said. "And you are now about to tell me how you ruined poor old Porter. Begin at the beginning."

"It was summer. We'd just got our bikes — but nowhere to race 'em, see. Short of time, I was in with my Old Man then — a slave-driver if ever there was one, Greg had his job, Colin had his homework. There wasn't time to get to the Brakeland and the only other place was that stretch of road by Porter's place. And he turned nasty. Used to come out and shout and wave his fists. And we'd laugh and shout back and give him the old Harvey. So then the police laid out one of their traps. Good flat stretch of road and after eight nobody on it, but controlled at 50 m.p.h. So they had us on that. Like I said before, people don't like motor-bikes. Maximum fine. And we'd none of us got it, just then. But I knew where to get it."

"Yes; you mugged your own mother!"

"We didn't *hurt* her. And we didn't take much. Just enough. But I got the boot. And we all had it in for old Porter."

"So you set fire to his chicken-house. Or organised it. Very cleverly. Despite the fact that revenge offered motive, it was never brought home to you. How was it done?"

"Dead easy! There was a girl. Crazy about animals, including hens. Talked about it a lot. Factory farming she called it, hens in battery houses, calves in crates, pigs in hot-houses. She'd like to set fire to the lot, she said. So we said — Why not start on that place of Porter's, a broiler house if ever there was one. So she did. Sudden death, she said, and smoke kills before they feel anything. And a girl on a horse . . . We were in the clear; all out at Anders place, playing silly games. One of his sisters had a birthday . . ."

Julia Walpole. As Tom had said, defensively on that first evening, when all this began. "Neurotic as hell."

He'd seen her a time or two — Alice always liked Jenny to bring her friends home. Thin, dark, nervy, weighed down by the woes of the world, asking subscriptions for abandoned dogs, old or ill-used donkeys, bulls in Spain, seals off the Norfolk coast, guinea-pigs in laboratories.

Tom had never failed her; he had contributed when asked; signed his name occasionally. But, to be honest, he'd never fully approved of Julia as a friend for Jenny — herself soft-hearted. He knew — few men better — what horrors existed, what things were done and would — despite all efforts, continue to be done. Something he had learned to live with, that Jenny must learn to live with if she were to be happy, and above all else he had wanted her to be happy.

Once, indeed, he had said from a wish to comfort Jenny, after one of Julia's outbursts, "Look Honey, make a bit of allowance for Nature. No animal breeds in intolerable circumstances — that is a *known* fact. If those hens Julia went on and on about were as unhappy as she thinks they simply wouldn't lay eggs. Look at those Pandas — everything laid on and no result." Jenny had cheered up then and beaten him at Scrabble.

He remembered, but shoved the thought away.

"Porter didn't run a broiler house. He was one of the last to give his fowls free range. And he was not well-insured . . . Yes, I see. It was the realisation of what she had done — mistakenly — that drove poor Julia to drugs. And not content with that you must desecrate her grave!"

"That didn't hurt her," the boy said callously.

156

"It drove her mother demented."

"What demented Ma Walpole was the thought that somebody *knew*."

"Knew what?"

"What they'd been up to. Julia *had* been pregnant. Jerry or Phil, is debateable. Turned on Julia was pretty wild. Jerry would have married her; dead keen to. But that didn't suit Ma Walpole's book. Julia must stay at school, pass exams, go to college. So she whisked her off to some place and got rid of it. It was after that Julia went on the hard stuff and finished herself off."

And there was that telephone again. Checking up.

The girl's voice but deeper than Jenny's or the one that had so resembled Jenny's, "Mr Penfold, could you spare me a minute?"

Kate Dawson.

"Kate! Nobody more welcome. I was just about to make a cup of tea. I'll hold it back."

"Make it," she said. "I'm in Overby. I thought I'd better ring, in case you were resting or something."

Fiddle with the door of the cloakroom; set the radio to work. Plug in the kettle.

Kate was that bit older than Jenny; had passed the examination which poor Julia had failed, and which for Jenny was now postponed. Her reward had been a spanking new little mini-traveller which she drove with expertise. Tom had planned something of the same sort for Jenny. Once she could drive; a reward for passing, if she passed, a consolation if she should fail.

Kate was one of those long-legged girls whom the fashion in trousers and lumber jackets suited to perfection. She wore her dark hair cropped short. She'd once said, in this very room, "I'm enough like a horse, without sporting a mane!" And it was true, her face, too long and strong-boned was rather like a horse's. Opposites attract one another, and she had been Jenny's best friend.

Well-mannered, she asked after Jenny, and then, setting down her cup with a decisive gesture, said, "But that was not what I came to talk about. Mr Penfold, I have no wish to be offensive . . . But are you *for any reason*, protecting Terry Upworth? If you are, for whatever reason, don't mind telling me, he's scared the daylight out of me, more than once. And I don't scare easy."

"But Kate . . . I'm sorry but I can't make the connection. What could I protect young Upworth *from*? I hardly know him. I've bought petrol at his place, and on Saturday he serviced my car and very obligingly brought it back."

"And then, when you weren't looking, went off in it."

"Curiously enough, Inspector Henderson seemed to have conceived that idea. He came out, reassured himself that the car was in place, and incidentally, locked it up for me."

"He didn't conceive that idea," Kate said bluntly. "I sold it to him. Did you see him see it?"

"No."

"Then how do you know?"

"I trust Henderson."

"Oh, do you? So did I — once. Now I'm not so sure. As I say, I took him this idea and he said he'd act on it. Naturally I was anxious to know, and he's shut up like a clam; all the jargon — Confidential matter; no information available. This he says to me! And he's my father's friend. I think there's something funny going on."

"Such as?" She had refused a biscuit; now Tom offered his cigarette box.

"Thanks. I'll stick to my own." She had her own lighter, too, and flicked it competently.

"I'll start with Nancy. She's my oldest friend. We practically shared a rattle. I can't make her see straight about that boy. She's infatuated. The kind of thing that sounds all right in a book but is damned silly in real life. She goes to his place and cooks for his disgusting parties. She went on Saturday morning to dump some stuff, and saw Terry working on your car and he said something about bringing it back here. Later on, while she was cooking there was a telephone call. Man's voice, saying Terry was going to be out of circulation for a bit. What an expression! What would it mean to you?"

"Well — that he'd be away. Possibly gone to ground." That was what Tom had intended it to mean.

"Nancy wasn't worried until she found that he hadn't said a word to anybody, not even to Greg as they call him — the one he always leaves in charge. Then somebody noticed that that precious bike of his was still in the workshop. Now Terry going anywhere without his bike is as inconceivable as the Arab without his steed. So Nancy began to worry and by Monday was sure something had happened to Terry. She knows how *I* feel about *him*, on the other hand I'm the only one who knows what goes on, so I got the lot. And then it did occur to me . . ." Kate Dawson had — like the horse she resembled — beautiful eyes, but of a greenish colour, perfect for the expression of malice. "I worked it out. It was entirely unlike him to do anybody a favour; he never did anybody a favour in his life. To catch a bus, or cadge a lift he'd have to get from here to the main road, and he never walked a step if he could help it. I thought it likely that he'd taken your car. And if he had . . . God," she spoke violently, "if he could only be put away, even for a fortnight; the whole bloody thing would fold."

"Dear me, Kate," Tom said, playing innocent, "you do seem to have it in for that young man."

"Why not? He ruined my life. Oh, I know I said Nancy was infatuated. I wasn't quite like that. And I didn't share a rattle with Colin — Colin Anders — but I'd been in love with him since we went to Miss Davie's kindergarten. This may sound absurd to you, Mr Penfold, but it can happen; it happened to us. We more or less pledged our troth when we were about twelve. Plain as rice pudding; he was to follow in his father's footsteps, I in Daddy's and have children, live happily ever after. Bourgeoise as hell — forgive the dirty word. But it worked until Colin fell in with the Upworth boy. Mind you, I knew that Colin wasn't very tough, but I am, which may be the wrong way round, but workable. I'd have done any spanking that was needed, with these, mythical children. I sound like Barrie, or Kipling,

160

don't I, but it was real. I knew, for instance, that Colin would never make a surgeon; just an ordinary, good sound GP. We'd both have been doing a useful job. And Terry Upworth killed the thing dead."

She scowled fiercely at the tip of her cigarette.

"You know what happened to Colin."

"Yes. Not from Jenny." He did not wish Kate to think Jenny a tittle-tattle. "I'm sorry, Kate."

"I'm furious! I fought so hard. I still go hot when I think of the things I stooped to, pandering to that little horror, bribing him not to supply Colin. Colin had a chance, then, and he was trying. And of course having a doctor for a father was a help. It was naive of me, I suppose. Terry never intended to keep his word. All he wanted was to make me jump through hoops. Getting power over people is all he thinks about."

Bits of the puzzle were falling into place. Fix up a foursome for me . . . Get me a picture of her . . .

"Knowing what you obviously do, why didn't you take more direct action to put Upworth out of business?"

"Well may you ask! Two reasons. As I told you, I was scared. Terry knew how I felt — he'd have guessed who had blabbed, and he'd have involved me. You see, I had been to one of his horrible parties. I had been seen dining in public with him. You can imagine how my parents would have felt! Also, Daddy's a lawyer. Have you ever asked yourself how much of a solicitor's income is derived from property changing hands? Conveyancing. Mortgages. Old Upworth is a client most lawyers would give their left arm for. Not that

161

he'd have minded. He told Terry to go to Hell. But his mother! Tigress defending her cub! And she's the one who counts. She can *write*."

"Can't Upworth?"

"Clamping his tongue firmly between his teeth," Kate said cruelly, "and handling a pen like a trowel, he can sign his name."

"I see. So you hoped the boy had taken my car and would do a spell in Borstal?"

"All modern amenities and psychiatrists on call," Kate said with a brief, bleak grin. "The point is, none of the rest could run it for a fortnight. Terry Upworth wouldn't tolerate any underling with brains. At least," she was anxious to be fair, "there's one intellectual type. A homosexual."

"And now you doubt Inspector Anderson's integrity. Can you tell me why?"

"Partly his behaviour to me. And his snuffing round for some mysterious foreigner. He even asked Daddy if he'd had anything to do with selling or leasing a pretty substantial property — or indeed any other dealings with a man of foreign origin."

Henderson had indeed left no stone unturned.

"That may not seem significant to you, Mr Penfold. It speaks volumes to me. Whether Terry Upworth took your car or not may seem irrelevant; but it drew Henderson's attention, and up goes the smokescreen. *Somebody else to blame.* Absolutely true to pattern. Shall I tell how it looks from where I stand?"

"Pray do."

162

"There was a leak. Terry knew and took off. I saw a chance and alerted Uncle Hendry — that's what I've always called him. Then I think he was got at, bought off. After all, you know, the police are not very well paid."

"Kate, you appall me."

"I appall myself at times. Would you mind if I looked in your garage. I still think . . ."

"By all means." He handed her the garage key. And, like Henderson, she came back, disappointed at finding the car there.

"Well," she said, "I'm sorry for bothering you and blurting out all my grudges and woes. I just hoped to see it ended, before I left."

"You are leaving, Kate. Holiday?"

"I'm going to Katmandu. I was dithering with the idea. All this has made me decide. I'm opting out. For the simple life. All this is too complicated for me."

"I think you are making a grave mistake. Kate, I know. I have lived and worked in pretty primitive places. The problems are the same; and sometimes worse. Do think again. Look, I was once on a job in Persia — when I was a whole man. We were building a sugar factory, and a bit of railway. We lived in caravans. We all got some sort of dysentry — twelve times in a night, out into a field and leeches, Kate, leeches, fastening on to every inch of . . . exposed flesh. You could loosen them — the end of a burning cigarette made them break their hold, and you'd no sooner dealt with them all — a contortionist act — than out into the field again, to acquire another lot."

163

Of this grossly humiliating aspect of life in strange places he had never spoken, even to Alice, as for Jenny . . . Bowels turned to water and pain, pain; bared buttocks, parasites — quite unthinkable. But to this girl . . .

"Kate, you'd hate it. Katmandu is further east than Persia, and even more primitive. I really think you should think again. Look, would you like to see a goat or a sheep skinned *alive* simply because a skin taken from a live animal was slightly larger and considerably more pliable than a skin taken from a dead one? All those coats, so prettily embroidered on the outside, so cosy within — that is their origin! I know it *sounds* all mystical, the temple bells a-ringing and the true Buddhist unwilling to tread on a beetle. All rubbish, Kate; they hold out their begging bowls to those who have skinned goats alive and made a few pence. How else could they live? I know how you feel — get away from it all, but don't go pitching yourself into filth and squalor."

"What else have I lived with lately? You don't know half . . ."

Tuesday, February 7th

"All right," Tom said at length. "I think that is all I need to know." He backed slightly and again fiddled with the door-stop. "Now we will talk about tomorrow."

"You promised to turn me loose."

"I shall do that. I'd like you to understand what this has all been about. At least, not all. I began with the desire to know the truth about my daughter — and to teach you a lesson. Later my interest widened."

He stooped and took from its hiding place the tape-recorder. As he did so he thought how strangely things worked out.

(The tape-recorder had been Doris' idea, she'd heard or read about such an article's place in every well-equipped office. So time-saving; Mr Penfold could dictate into it while she typed in the outer office; then while he was on his rounds she could run the tape and type from it. Easier than shorthand. To please her, since she seemed so set on it he had bought the machine though he did not see the real need for it. It had not been a successful experiment. Doris with a tape-recorder was, in fact, not unlike Alice with a car. The thing defied her. It went too fast, or too slow. The tape itself became tangled. They reverted to their old way of doing things, and then, because to her it was a symbol

165

of failure, Doris had taken against the thing itself. It was not much bigger than an ordinary brick, but somehow it was always in the way. So he'd brought it home.)

"I have here a record of all our talk in this room — except that fandango of lies concerning my daughter. Tomorrow I shall deposit it in a very safe place — not Mr Dawson's office or anywhere like that. I shall also make, in two separate places, a statement as to how this information was forced out of you. I shall also leave instructions. If some untimely accident should happen to me — I put nothing past you — this goes straight to the police. But — mark this — it will also go straight to the police if you do not, the moment you are free, disband your gang and stop this abominable traffic. Is that understood? Otherwise the only use I shall make of this information will be to drop a hint to the authorities about regular travellers being taken too much for granted."

On the whole, better than Terry had counted upon. The revelation about the recording was a bit of a shock. He'd always intended if ever he got out of here and the cripple dared to blab, to whip in a charge of illegal detention and of physical ill-usage. He had thought over Tom's remark about being a laughing stock; there'd been an accomplice — there must have been. And naturally he would deny having said any of the things which he had said. The taping of the talk rather altered that. However . . . the great thing was to get out of here.

"And how do I get out?"

Tom could have told him, in simple words which a child could have understood. But he thought of the havoc this loathsome boy had wrought; the ruined happiness of families that he now knew about — and there could be dozens, scores of others. Let him sweat it out a little longer.

"You'll see," he said. "I shall leave the house at my usual time, and within thirty minutes that thing —" he nodded towards the handcuff — "will release itself."

Terry simply did not believe it. For one thing he had the congenital liar's incapacity to believe; for another he had never bothered about anything which made the slightest demand upon intellect. Satellites whizzing about in space, but controlled from earth had never won a moment's interest from him. All he cared for was people, and for them only in so far as they could be manipulated by him.

The incipient hysteria upon which his unstable character was based leapt up and took control.

What this mother-fucking bastard meant to do was leave him here to starve. He had once threatened to, hadn't he? Then the accomplice would be called upon again — not this time to carry a living man into the house, but a dead one out of it. Didn't he have, working for him, a man who had done time for murder?

The handcuff was now only too familiar to him. Its smooth surface broken in two places, where it was attached to the chain, and where it bulged out into a protubance no bigger than a postage stamp, about as thick as a cigarette. It had on one of its longer sides a

167

series of perforations. Keyholes. And the key was in the cripple's pocket; on that ring.

Tom, showing the tape-recorder, had advanced into the cloakroom; his useless feet propped against the chair's footrest. It took no time at all for Terry to reach out and pull, and pull.

Even so, had Tom been the man he had been before this whole thing started, he could have held his own, so strong of hand and arm and shoulder. As it was, at the crucial moment, his hands failed, as they had over the plate of meat, the pan of ashes.

The struggle was brief.

Now, steady, Terry. It's one of the small keys. Several of them, still warm from contact with Tom's body.

Awkward job, working left-handedly. Try another. Try that one again. And this, and this. Upside down. Sideways.

It took some time for the truth to dawn. When it did the boy screamed and screamed.

Thursday, February 9th

Bugger all customers, the milkman said to himself as he saw the Wednesday's milk still on the step. They never bother to let you know. Exactly the same thing had happened with old Salter just along the lane, but he would have thought Mr Penfold would have been more considerate.

Friday, February 10th

Doris said, "Well, Jack I don't know. It's fish again. But somehow . . . He did say he was busy. And I noticed, when you got the milk out of the fridge, he'd got enough food for a week. I'd say leave it. What about Chesford tomorrow? On their home ground and with a decent referee?"

"Bet you five pee," Jack said. No need to say which way; Doris always bet on her boys.

Saturday, February 11th

"Will you stop being so bloody daft," Josh Salter asked, grabbing his beloved by the collar which she now always wore. "There's nobody there." No light in any window. No sign of life at all. And who could blame the poor fellow? Hard enough to be on your own when you were spry and lively, and had a good dog for company. "You go on like this, Gyp and it'll mean the lead."

Mrs Cooper, walking her own dog in the last of the light, noted with approval that the horrible old man was making some slight effort to keep his horrible dog under control. So she tendered the typical English sign of approval — a remark about the weather. "Days drawing out," she said. And it was true. Streaks of yellow in the evening sky promised daffodils; other streaks, pale apple green promised young leaves.

Against this pretty background, the Old Barn looked very dark and bleak and lonely. But she hardened her heart. Mr Penfold had not properly appreciated her good services. Let him eat fish fingers!

Sunday, February 12th

"Well, thank you for trying," Alice said to the pleasant young man who from some deep cave operated something called Ship-to-Shore, used mainly by the very rich. Alice was temporarily very rich — she had joined a Bingo game and won fifteen pounds, no less. She wanted to hear Tom's voice, to be assured that he was all right, to tell him that Jenny had made a wonderful recovery and was at this very moment taking part in some Fancy Dress thing.

But she had obviously got the time wrong. Clocks went forward — or was it back? And she'd muddled it. Tom must be at the Works.

Monday, February 13th

Higgins said, "Get the Exchange, Doris. There's some fault in the line. He must be there. Where else could he be? And there was a high wind, Saturday."

Doris dialled, spoke, listened. And then, holding the receiver at an angle, said, "There's nothing reported. Nothing out of order. But no answer. My God, Mr Higgins! He did say something about an invention. S'pose it blew up in his face!"

Not very eagerly, Higgins said, "Maybe I should go and take a look."

"I'll come," Doris said, snatching up her head scarf. "Being around with the boys so much, I do know a bit of First Aid."

Higgins ran a lively little car and he drove fast. Front door bell, a musical chime; back door bell a kind of buzz.

"Nothing for it," Higgins said. "Must break in. He could have turned that blasted chair over. Lend us that scarf, Doris."

Cautiously wrapping his hand he broke a pane of the french window in the living-room, reached in, unlocked it and entered. Across the room, into the hall, following his nose — his nose . . .

What he saw he did not understand, but he realised that Doris was close behind him, and as soon as he saw what he saw he said, "Doris, go away. Go sit in the car." No sight for even a tough girl, a resolute Chesford supporter. "There's nothing you can do," Higgins said, summing the whole thing up in words as cogent and urgent as any words ever uttered by man. "This is a job for the police . . ."

Also available in ISIS Large Print:

The Haunting of Gad's Hall

Norah Lofts

No one dared reveal the truth about the haunting of Gad's hall.

No one at Gad's Hall could admit what they knew about the room in the attic. The locked room that held the Thorley family's most shameful secret. The terrifying room that had once been the living tomb of a beautiful young woman possessed by the darkest evil. Years had passed but the relentless diabolic force abided — waiting until it could once again possess an innocent and inflict its horror upon the living. It was a force countless centuries old. It was simply a matter of time before it would strike again. And when the Spender family moved into Gad's Hall, that time had come . . .

ISBN 978-0-7531-8558-2 (hb)
ISBN 978-0-7531-8559-9 (pb)

ISIS publish a wide range of books in large print, from fiction to biography. Any suggestions for books you would like to see in large print or audio are always welcome. Please send to the Editorial Department at:

ISIS Publishing Limited
7 Centremead
Osney Mead
Oxford OX2 0ES

A full list of titles is available free of charge from:

Ulverscroft Large Print Books Limited

(UK)
The Green
Bradgate Road, Anstey
Leicester LE7 7FU
Tel: (0116) 236 4325

(Australia)
P.O. Box 314
St Leonards
NSW 1590
Tel: (02) 9436 2622

(USA)
P.O. Box 1230
West Seneca
N.Y. 14224-1230
Tel: (716) 674 4270

(Canada)
P.O. Box 80038
Burlington
Ontario L7L 6B1
Tel: (905) 637 8734

(New Zealand)
P.O. Box 456
Feilding
Tel: (06) 323 6828

Details of ISIS complete and unabridged audio books are also available from these offices. Alternatively, contact your local library for details of their collection of ISIS large print and unabridged audio books.

A Wayside Tavern

Norah Lofts

A Wayside Tavern tells the story of a Suffolk drinking place from the end of the Roman occupation of Britain, until the present day. The Roman veteran, crippled and left behind, worshipped Mithras, so the place became known as the One Bull and down through the centuries it accommodated itself to changing times and became a clearing house for contraband, a miniature Hell Fire Club, a fashionable hotel, a mere pub.

Closely connected, indeed just across the yard, was the church of St Cerdic, king and martyr, who fought the Danes and was once famous for the miracles performed at his shrine. His remains were lost in the Reformation but something remained and some people who stood on the site of his tomb experienced a change of heart.

Inside the inn, despite all external changes, one passion raged — to retain possession.

ISBN 978-0-7531-8332-8 (hb)
ISBN 978-0-7531-8333-5 (pb)

Anna, Where Are You?

Patricia Wentworth

Thomasina Elliott never expected to keep in touch with lonely orphan Anna Ball after they left school. However when Anna wrote to her, she felt obliged to reply. The correspondence between them was constant for years until Thomasina found herself waiting for a letter that never came.

Thomasina has no particular reason to believe that anything has happened to her old friend, but when she makes some enquiries she discovers Anna has disappeared without a trace. Deeply concerned, Thomasina turns to Detective Inspector Frank Abbott, who asks Miss Silver to investigate.

ISBN 978-0-7531-8122-5 (hb)
ISBN 978-0-7531-8123-2 (pb)

Gad's Hall

Norah Lofts

There were no screams in the night, no objects flying through the air, no murderous, disembodied voices — but Gad's Hall was haunted just the same.

For the Spender family, the ancient, beautifully kept house had seemed a godsend, an incredible bargain, almost a gift from its owner — a kindly man who merely wanted someone to protect the family homestead, to make Gad's come alive again.

And it did. Soon a strong-willed, sensible woman would be overtaken by irrational feelings she could not control, all because of the unspeakable secret kept by the women who had lived at Gad's Hall more than a century ago . . .

Rich in historical detail, suspense and romance, Gad's Hall subtly entices us into the realm of the supernatural with the tale of a house forever doomed by a young girl's powerful obsession.

ISBN 978-0-7531-7942-0 (hb)
ISBN 978-0-7531-7943-7 (pb)

Bless This House

Norah Lofts

The house was built in the Old Queen's time - built for an Elizabethan pirate who was knighted for the plunder he brought home. It survived many eras, many reigns - it saw the passing of Cromwell and the Civil War. It became rich with an Indian Nabob and poor with a twentieth century innkeeper. It saw wars, and lovers, and death. Children were born there, both heirs and bastards. It had ghosts and legends and a history that grew stranger with every generation.

The house was Merravay - and its story stretched over four hundred years . . .

ISBN 978-0-7531-7569-9 (hb)
ISBN 978-0-7531-7570-5 (pb)